MW01120937

Ocean's Lure

Ocean's Lure

Tim Covell

Somewhat Grumpy Press Inc.

Copyright © 2021 by Tim Covell

Cover design and photo by Tim Covell
Edited by Georgia Atkin

All rights reserved. No part of this book may be reproduced in any manner whatsoever without written permission except in the case of brief quotations embodied in critical articles and reviews. It is illegal to copy this book, post it to a website, or distribute it by any other means without permission. Tim Covell asserts the moral right to be identified as the author of this work.

Any brand names or product names used in this book are trade names, service marks, trademarks or registered trademarks of their respective owners. The author and publisher are not associated with any product or vendor mentioned in this book. None of any companies referenced within the book have endorsed the book.

This novel is entirely a work of fiction. The names, characters, and incidents portrayed in it are either the work of the author's imagination or used in a fictitious manner. Any resemblance to actual persons, living or dead, events, or localities is entirely coincidental.

ISBN
978-1-9992884-7-1 (paperback)
978-1-9992884-8-8 (eBook)

First Printing, April 2021
Second Printing, June 2021

CONTENTS

v

ACKNOWLEDGEMENT

I wrote the first draft of this novel ten years ago, as a NaNoWriMo project. Since then, many people encouraged me and suggested story improvements. To name just a few: Dorothyanne Brown, Tanya Benoit, Janet Brush, Stu Ducklow, Renee Field, Beth Irvine, Magi Nams, Ella Dodson, Sue Slade, Suzanne Atkinson, Donna Alward, Nikki McIntosh, and Michelle Helliwell.

Thanks to everyone at Romance Writers of Atlantic Canada, my blog readers, Facebook friends, and classmates at University of Calgary Continuing Education. Thanks also to my editor, Georgia Atkin. I appreciate all the support from so many people, but I admit being too stubborn to accept every suggestion, and the last hands on the book were mine, so I'm solely responsible for the content, including any remaining typos and plot holes.

1

Chapter 1

Cape Breton, Nova Scotia, Fall 2015

"It's going to be that kind of day, isn't it?"

Marianna turned the kitchen faucet off, then on again. No water flowed. She tried twisting it from hot to cold and back, not expecting that to help. It didn't.

"Great, no water," she said to herself. "Lunch will have to wait."

The day had started with an email from the Wilsons, cancelling their reservation. A week's stay would have been a good boost to her campground's October income. Then she'd received a loan payment overdue notice in the mail. When she phoned the finance company, they had assured her the notice was a mistake, and they had received all the payments since June on time, but they couldn't explain why they had sent the notice. And now the water was out.

She had an alternate water supply for the house, and bottled water for campers, but no water meant no showers. She glanced out the side window. Sheila and Barry, her only guests last night, were approaching her house. They did not look happy.

She went out to the deck to meet them. Working face to face with customers, especially unhappy ones, was Marianna's least favourite part of the job. During the summer, Riley dealt with customers. Now Riley was down in Halifax at university. Marianna reminded herself that the customer was always right. These customers more than most. Barry was a prolific Tripadvisor reviewer, under his own name, and Sheila had a large Instagram following. They didn't demand discounts, but never missed a chance to remind Marianna of their followers. The usual conversation was compliment, complaint, reminder.

As they drew close, Marianna put on her best how-can-I-help-you smile and walked down the steps to the ground. Cerebus, Marianna's Airedoodle, rushed past her with his tail wagging and greeted the couple.

"Good morning Sheila, Barry. Did you have a good night?"

"Wonderful," said Sheila. She petted Cerebus. "I fell asleep to the sound of the waves. No better way to sleep. Well, almost no better way." She kissed her husband of three days. "The morning hasn't been so good, though. The water ran out during my morning shower. I'm hoping you can fix that before I have to post pictures of myself looking like this. It would shock my followers."

Marianna thought Sheila looked like she had just stepped out of a spa, but only nodded. "I'm looking into the water now. It should be back on soon."

"Your location is fabulous," said Barry, "and the fall colours are amazing. It would be a shame if something like unreliable water detracted from an otherwise positive review."

"After tonight's dinner, I'm sure the review will be great."

"Yes, we are looking forward to that," said Sheila. "We hope the rain holds off until tomorrow, after we've packed up. Can we take Cerebus for a beach walk?"

"Sure, he'd love that. Go with them, Cere." She watched them walk away, Sheila beside Cerebus, and Barry walking behind them. He stopped and took a picture of the tree-covered hill at the back of the campground. Sheila glanced back but kept walking. So much for the honeymoon period, Marianna thought, and then decided she was being too cynical. It was better than those couples that would not let go of each other, as if a strong gust of wind might end the relationship. She thought of Troy, always taking her hand when they walked together, saying he never wanted to miss a chance to touch her. Which would have been charming if he had seen her more often. So, holding hands is not any better than not holding hands. There's just no pleasing me, she thought. Oh yes there is—she smiled at a memory—just not in relationships.

She climbed the hill to the well house, hoping the problem was minor, and that nothing else would go wrong today. She wanted tonight's dinner for Barry and Sheila to be a success and help promote the campground. She reviewed a mental checklist of the supplies and preparation required. Apart from the logistics of transporting everything to the beach and back, the dinner was easy. As for weather, the morning sun was warm, and the sky clear. If the forecast cold front came in as planned, there would be cloud cover to keep the day's heat into the evening. Too early, and it would rain; too late, and it would be cold. I can't control the weather, she reminded herself.

The well house was on the highest point of her land. Before

going in, she turned to look down across the campground and out to the open ocean. After two years, she still found the view breathtaking. Her mother had said she was crazy to leave Toronto for the northern shore of Cape Breton Island, but Marianna knew this was where she belonged. In the country, on this property, by herself. She watched as an eagle swooped down from a nearby tree, flew out over the ocean, dived into the water, and flew up again with a fish in its talons.

* * *

Dylan stopped the truck when the road turned into a wharf. He was lost. He could not possibly be lost in a town with five streets, but none of them were Johnson Hill Road. His phone had guided him to Bay St. Lawrence, on the northern tip of Cape Breton Island, but now it said he had arrived, even though he was not at any campground or beach. He looked out the window at a street sign. He was apparently on Government Wharf Road, clearly on the wharf section. The GPS said he was on Main Street. A few fishing boats were parked, or docked, or whatever the proper term was, on one side, and an aging warehouse was on the other, all doors closed. No one was around, and an abandoned pickup truck was the only vehicle in sight. Dylan reversed until the road widened, made a U-turn, and drove back to the Co-op store. There was no sign of Johnson Hill Road, which should have been next to the parking lot. The directions on his phone were clear: turn right onto Johnson Hill, just past the Co-op. However, there were only driveways for the houses, spaced irregularly on the large lots.

He pulled into the Co-op parking lot, climbed out of the rental SUV, and walked across the hard-packed gravel. From the outside, the Co-op looked like an old-fashioned general store. The inside confirmed that impression. Besides shelves of food and snacks, there were local carvings and hooked rugs hanging on a wall, and rakes and snow shovels by the door. Dylan looked over the section of camping supplies but didn't see anything else he needed. He had stopped at a Canadian Tire and a Sobeys on the way from the airport and purchased everything he needed to look like a camper for three days.

The store had a food counter beside the cash, with an empty pizza warming cabinet, and a sign promising Fresh Sandwiches Made to Order. That, and the smell of roasted chicken, reminded him he hadn't eaten lunch, he'd been up since four, and it was almost two in the afternoon. He rang the bell on the counter, expecting a grizzled, tobacco-chewing old-timer to appear.

"Be right out." A teenager, with blue hair and a Pink Floyd T-shirt, slipped through the curtain behind the cash. "Sorry to keep you waiting, sir. What can I get for you?"

"What sandwiches do you have?"

"Sorry, just chicken today. It's still warm, if that's okay. We could do an egg sandwich too. Or tuna."

"Warm chicken would be great, thanks. To go, please."

The teen turned and yelled back through the curtain, "Chicken sandwich, Ma." She turned back to Dylan. "It'll be right out. Can you pay cash? The card machine's not working."

He paid and asked for directions to the Sandcastle Rock Campground.

"Just turn right onto Johnson Hill Road and keep going. You can't miss it. Only thing on the road, and it ends there. About twenty kilometres."

"Where's Johnson Hill Road?"

"Just after the parking lot. Right there." The teen pointed to the parking lot.

"That's not a driveway? It's not paved, and there's no sign."

"Nope. That's the road. It looks like it goes to McNeil's garage, but the road goes left just before that. Marianna wants to put up signs for the road and her campground, but there's new rules about road signs, and she can't. Here's your sandwich."

A woman Dylan assumed was the teen's mother came through the curtain, holding a paper bag. She handed it to Dylan, smiled, and said, "Here you go, dear." It was the third time he'd been called *dear* today, and he had this odd feeling of coming home. He'd left the province over ten years ago, hadn't been back, and never missed it. Even when he lived in Nova Scotia, he'd never been north of Halifax, and then only once, when he hitchhiked to Toronto. Cape Breton, at the north end of Nova Scotia, was as unknown as whatever was north of the last subway stop on the Yonge Street line in Toronto.

"Thanks." The bag was heavy for a sandwich. He opened it, and saw the sandwich, made with a bun, a large dill pickle wrapped in plastic, and an apple. "I just paid for a sandwich."

"It's all included," said the older lady. "Enjoy your visit, and tell Marianna that Susan and Wendy, that's my girl," Susan indicated the teenager, "say hi. You'll like Marianna. She can be prickly at first, but she's a lovely young woman."

A few minutes later, Dylan was driving along what appeared to be Johnson Hill Road. He realized he hadn't asked why there was no street sign. It didn't matter. It didn't matter that Marianna was a lovely young woman, either. He was here to do a job. It wasn't a pleasant job, but it would make a lot of money for his company and secure his future. Marianna wouldn't be happy, but she knew the risk when she signed the loan agreement.

2

∽

Chapter 2

Marianna unlocked the door, entered the well house, and turned on the light. It worked. So far, so good. Piping and tanks filled the windowless room. Glowing green indicator lights and no water on the floor suggested the problem was not major, but it was not obvious either. She unplugged a rechargeable flashlight and used it to check the breakers and pressure gauges. The power was good for all pumps and the ultraviolet filter, but the different pressures at different points suggested a clogged filter. She aimed the flashlight at each one. None of them looked bad or were due for replacement. She'd need to shut off the pumps, release system pressure, and check them one at a time. At least she had a good stock of spare filters.

The well house was cool and dank. She stepped outside for a moment to enjoy the sun and fresh air. On the beach below the campground, Sheila was throwing sticks for Cerebus. At the other end of the beach, Barry was taking pictures of the eagle. Movement off to the side caught her eye, and she saw a red SUV heading into the campground and down towards her house. She was not expecting anyone and had forgotten to put a sign up at the house, so she'd have to go down. She closed the well house door, sighed, and started back down the hill.

The SUV pulled up at the house, and the driver got out. He looked around, knocked at the door, and peered in the windows. She waved, and yelled "Hello," but he was not looking in her direction and could not hear her over the surf. He went back to his truck and honked the horn. Jerk, she thought, and waved again. This time he noticed her and waved back.

Tall, with short black hair, and dressed in preppy shorts and a polo shirt that revealed pale but muscular limbs. A gym rat, she thought, just like Troy. As she got closer, she guessed he was in his late twenties. She wondered what brought him here. She couldn't see anyone else through the luxury SUV's tinted windows, but no one else was getting out, so he was probably alone. Solo campers were rare, and attractive young solo campers very rare. The bicycle tourists, with their tanned muscular bodies, were a mix of young men and men trying to prove themselves younger than they were, though if they made it to her campground, they were in decent shape. The wanderers, of all ages, driving rundown camper vans, sometimes toting an instrument, told great stories but too often assumed they were charming enough to share her bed. They were almost always wrong.

The new arrival smiled as she approached, revealing perfect teeth. Of course.

"Hi. I'm Marianna. Welcome to Sandcastle Rock Campground."

"Good afternoon. Dylan." He offered his hand, and she shook it. His palm was warmer than she expected, or perhaps the weather was cooler than she realized after her trek up and back from the well house. "Sorry to disturb you." He waved at the nearly empty campground. "Are you closed for the season?"

"No, I'm open until mid-October, but after the Labour Day weekend it's much quieter, especially during the week. Just one couple here today. But you have your choice of sites, and no close neighbours. Did you want to look around and decide if you are going to stay?" She hoped he would.

"No, this is where I want to be. It looks just like the picture on the website. That's a well-designed site, by the way." His brown eyes seemed sincere and warm.

"Thanks. I made it myself. That's what I do. Make websites. When I'm not camping. When it's slow here, or in the off-season." Marianna cursed herself for being flustered. He was cute enough, and he had given her a compliment, but that should hardly be enough to make her weak at the knees. However, it had been months since she had enjoyed a special guest. Special guest sounded better than one-night stand. Whatever she called it, it was her turf, her rules, and usually her pleasure. Regardless, they'd be gone within a day or two, with no awkwardness or emotional entanglement. Dylan was cute enough to be a special guest and seemed obnoxious enough for her to bid him goodbye without regrets. She took a breath. "How many nights will you be staying? Though you don't need to decide now. There's lots of room, obviously."

"Three nights should do it, I think."

"Exploring the trail?" The Cabot Trail was a picturesque drive around Cape Breton Island. It could be done in a day, but side trips and exploring the national park that covered a good part of the island could add days to the drive. There were over two dozen trails to waterfalls and spectacular views. His leather boat shoes and Calvin Klein dress socks did not suggest he did much hiking.

"Yes, seeing the sights." But he looked down, then back at his SUV, avoiding her eyes. She wondered what his real interest in the area was. Not that it mattered much. She had learned that part of being a good host was to mind her own business.

This close, she could see no one else was in the truck. "So, three nights, one person, tent site. It's twenty dollars a night. That includes water and electric, though not all the sites have it. You can also get water and power here at the house, and at the washroom building over there. It looks under construction from here, but that's the picnic shelter addition. Go in on the other side. You can have any site you want, but the sites closer to the ocean and further up the hill don't have water or electricity. There's Wi-Fi, but only at the house."

"Sounds good. That's the cash price, right?" He winked.

Marianna bristled. "I declare my income and pay my taxes, sir, and it is the same price whether you want to pay by cash, credit, or debit." She stepped past him. "Would you mind coming into the office for a moment? There's a registration form, and I'll need to see your ID." She opened the front door of the house, and gestured for him to walk in.

He stepped behind her and took the door, putting his arm well above hers. This close, he towered over her, and she could smell him. His scent was a musky sandalwood. It was warm and earthy, not the spicy or bitter menthols sold as sporty fragrances that she expected.

"After you, Marianna, and please, call me Dylan. No offense

meant. When I stopped for breakfast, gas, and a few supplies, it was obvious other folks around here prefer cash."

She stepped inside and looked back at him, still holding the door.

"Thank you. Come in, don't let the flies in. Yes, I guess some folks around here make it plain they want cash." She turned and walked around behind the counter that took up most of the space. The small office at the front of the house had been a covered porch that she had enclosed. "Well, it's none of my business. I'm come-from-away, even though this was my grandmother's place."

Dylan followed her in and faced her across the counter. "The campground is that old?"

"No. She kept it as a small farm. I came here and started the campground two years ago. Before that it was called Johnson Hill Farm, though no one around here knew why. So, I didn't hurt anyone's feelings when I changed the name to Sandcastle Rock." He seemed taller in the office. Marianna was grateful for the counter between them. She was already telling him more than he needed to know. She concentrated on finding the camper registration form and reminded herself to add shortcut buttons to the camper database she had built.

"Why Sandcastle Rock?"

"There's a rock formation on the beach, near the bottom of the stairs. When I was little, I thought it was like a giant sandcastle, though it's only about two metres. Nothing like the flowerpot rocks over in New Brunswick. You can't see it until you reach the stairs to the beach."

"Two metres is impressive for a rock formation on a beach,

especially when there are no cliffs in the area." He looked out the windows across the empty campground. "Not very busy."

She started filling out the form and replied without looking up.

"After the Thanksgiving weekend, there is very little business. Lots of places close for the season, but I stay open until the end of the month." And hope for as many late visitors as possible. Starting the campground had been expensive, and this year she'd be lucky to break even, assuming the well did not need costly repairs. She tried to take control of the conversation. "How long have you been in Cape Breton, Dylan?"

"Just got here. I flew into Halifax first thing this morning and drove up. Came straight here to make sure I had a place to stay, and I'll explore the trail from here."

"It's a good location for that. Can I see your driver's licence please? Thanks." In the photo, he was wearing a white shirt and tie. His full name was Dylan Felder. He was twenty-eight, almost her age, and older than he looked. She recognized the Toronto address as a luxury condominium development close to downtown. It had been under construction when she left. "What brings you out here? Seeing the colours?"

"Yes. Looks like I got lucky and timed it just right. I'm looking forward to a couple of relaxing days. I like to get away from the office sometime, and get back to nature, leave behind the luxuries and rough it."

"You picked the right place, but with that truck, you don't look like you are roughing it."

"I suppose it is a little fancy. My admin assistant rented it for me."

Marianna handed back the driver's licence. "So, you are escaping the office for a few days? I can appreciate that. I used to live in Toronto myself."

"Really? What brought you out here?" asked Dylan.

"Various things." Marianna caught herself before she went down that path. "This is a long way to come to see fall colours and get back to nature. I'm sure there are places that are closer to Toronto than my campground."

"I used to go up into cottage country, but I enjoy discovering new places, so the last few years I've been exploring the east coast. The colours on Cape Breton Island got great reviews, and so did your campground."

"Thanks, that's good to know. Have you been up here before?"

"No. This is the first time I've crossed the Canso Causeway. Last time I stayed at Ocean Front near Antigonish." He pronounced it anti-gonish instead of an-tigo-nish, which left her doubting he'd ever been there. Or maybe, like Troy, he assumed he was always correct.

Marianna printed out the registration receipt and handed it to Dylan. He seemed unfamiliar with the registration process. If you're a camper, I'm the queen, she thought. She wondered what he was hiding, or if he was boasting about camping and his travels to impress her. She could live with that. "You can set up anywhere you like. Did you want any help setting up?"

"No thanks, I'm good. No sites are reserved for anybody, then? How do you stay in business with only a few customers a night?"

"Good management." Marianna gave Dylan a thin-lipped smile and was pleased to see his apologetic expression. He started to speak, and she interrupted. "One other thing.

There's no water right now. A problem with the well. It should be working in an hour or two, but meanwhile I've got some bottled water at the house. Just help yourself. It's in the porch at the side door. There's a rain barrel and a bucket for flushing the toilet at the bathhouse. Just no showers."

"Waiting for a plumber, out here?"

"I'm taking care of it," said Marianna.

"I know a little plumbing myself, so if you need help, I'd be happy to assist."

Marianna tensed at his assessment of her capabilities and looked again at his manicured hands. "I can take care of it. You are on vacation. It's a little chilly for swimming, but a walk on the beach can be lovely, and there are some hiking trails. There's a map on the side wall of the house just outside this door. There's also Wi-Fi there. Anywhere near this computer. The Wi-Fi's slow, but fine for email."

"Thanks. I'll probably just set up and take it easy this afternoon. Perhaps walk along the beach, or maybe a nap. It's been a long day."

"One more thing." Marianna realized another possible benefit of Dylan's visit. "Are you eating dinner at the campground tonight? I'm doing a lobster bake on the beach tonight for the newlyweds—the couple here. Perhaps you could join us?"

"Sounds delightful, but is there enough food for an unexpected guest?"

"Yes. A fisher from Bay St. Lawrence is bringing the lobsters by this afternoon. I just need to get an extra one."

"Will twenty cover it?" Dylan pulled his wallet from his back pocket.

"No charge. But I could use a little help lugging things to the beach and back?"

"Sure." Dylan grinned, though she wasn't sure if he was amused by the invitation or how she'd roped him into helping. "I'll go set the tent up, and have that walk, then come back here?"

"Take your time. If you could meet me here at five-thirty?"

Dylan nodded and left the office.

Marianna set off for the well. His help would make the dinner easier, and she'd spend some time with him tonight. Their conversation confirmed he was confident enough to be decent if not great in bed, and he was annoying enough that she would not miss him when he left.

Halfway up to the well house, she turned back. Sheila and Barry were sitting on the beach, side by side, both looking out to the ocean. Cerebus was sleeping near them. Dylan was setting up his tent at the lowest part of the campground, close to the beach. He seemed to be having trouble with the tent and was reading the instructions. "Who are you and why are you here?" she wondered. "Are you another of today's problems, or are things looking up?" The next time she looked down, the tent was set up, and Dylan was reading a book on the picnic table.

* * *

Assembling the tent proved easier than the instructions had suggested. Between the dressy clothes and the flashy truck, being almost the only person at the campground, and being snappy to his host, Dylan's plan to blend in and quietly observe the place was not working very well. On the other hand, finding a reason to call in the loan would be much easier than he had expected. It was no wonder she had missed payments. Business was terrible, and the lack of water suggested poor maintenance and high repair bills. The gorgeous young redhead who owned the place was a little feisty, but also foolish, giving away free lobster to guests. Her ability to fight or pay the loan cancellation looked minimal.

With the tent finished, he picked up the spy thriller he'd found at the airport. His story of wanting to escape the office wouldn't work if he spent all his time on his laptop, not that he could do much without Wi-Fi. Not offering Wi-Fi at every site probably cost her customers. However, it had been a long time since he'd had the chance to do nothing but read. Too long.

Dylan sat at his site's picnic table, facing the ocean. The surf was noisier than he expected, but not unpleasant. A shift in the wind brought salty air, and memories of long ago. He and his sister had spent many afternoons at the beach near their house. He hadn't realized he missed the salt air. He'd walked along the waterfront in Toronto, but without awareness of how dull the lake was compared to the ocean. But there was decent Wi-Fi along the Toronto waterfront. He tried to avoid further comparisons by paying attention to the book.

The story opened with an explosion during a bank robbery, and within two pages revealed that the robbery was staged to cover a major fraud. From the little Dylan knew about the land deal planned for Marianna's campground, the topic was too close to home. The next chapter was a kinky sex scene, introducing the detective investigating the fraud, but neither the explicit sex nor the over-complicated backstory held Dylan's interest. He considered a walk, then decided a nap was the best option. He stood up and scanned the hill above the campground for Marianna. She was not visible, but the door to the well house was open. She's a hard worker, he thought.

He crawled into his tent, set his phone alarm for five, and reclined on his sleeping bag. The ground that had looked flat when he set up the tent turned out to slope to one side. He tried facing downhill, but his head was lower than his feet. He crawled around so he was still facing downhill, but his head was higher. That worked. He closed his eyes and listened to the waves. She hears this every night, he thought. Will she miss it? Should he care?

3

Chapter 3

Dylan woke refreshed and less sore than he expected from sleeping on the ground. The sun had warmed the little tent, and he felt the need for a shower before being in polite company. From the tent, he could see the well house door was closed. Hopefully Marianna had fixed the water. He gathered clothes and his bathroom kit.

There was plenty of hot running water, and the bathroom was spotlessly clean. It was also private, not the communal men's room he had expected. The bathroom building contained four small private two-piece bathrooms, and four large bathrooms that included double showers. Family friendly, he thought, looking around the room as he dried himself after a refreshing shave and shower. His parents had been too poor for vacations, but sometimes a friend's parents took him camping for a weekend. The trips had been fun times, but the places were run down compared to this. He dressed in the best clothes he had brought, black chinos and a red patterned short-sleeve dress shirt. He returned to his tent to drop off his bathroom kit and clothes and headed for the house to meet Marianna.

On the way, he met the newlyweds, coming back from a walk. He would have known they were newlyweds, even if Marianna had not told him. It was obvious in their attention to each other as they walked towards him, though they were not holding hands. A large dog with curly brown fur trotted over to him.

"Good afternoon, fellow camper," said the man. "We're Barry and Sheila Pender, from Ottawa. This is Cerebus, but he's not ours. Belongs to Marianna. He's friendly, no need to fear him." He leaned in closer. "Friendlier than she is, but she's a decent sort."

Cerebus was sniffing Dylan's legs and crotch. Dylan backed away. "I'm not scared of him, but I don't like dogs, and don't want him to lick me. I just put on clean pants."

Sheila called Cerebus to her, and she petted him.

"Thanks. I'm Dylan, from Toronto. I understand you are just married. Congratulations."

"Thanks." They both beamed. "And I can't think of a better place for a honeymoon, can you?" Dylan could think of dozens of places that would be better for a honeymoon but agreed with Barry. "Indeed. Gorgeous here. How did you discover it?"

"We do a lot of camping, but this place is new. We thought we'd check it out—new material for our followers. Sheila here is an influencer, and I'm a travel writer. Some reviews, some freelance," said Barry. "The place is a little rough around the edges, but that's part of its little country charm. What brought you here?"

"Oh, the usual. Looking for a quiet place to spend a few days."

"It's certainly quiet here. But it will be busier after we've finished our postings," said Barry. "Most campgrounds these days are parking lots for motor homes. Nice to see somewhere set up for tent campers."

"True," Dylan said, though he knew motor homes were the most profitable visitors to campgrounds. Marianna's large tent sites could accommodate motor homes or trailers, and she was offering premium tent sites at regular rates. "I understand she's doing a lobster boil for you tonight."

"Bake. Yes, she's doing a lobster bake for us, can you believe it?" asked Sheila. "The pictures will be fabulous. I've added so many followers since we've been here." Sheila tugged on Barry's arm. "Let's not be late for dinner. We still need to change, and I need to do something with my hair. Dylan, you're coming too, right?"

"Yes. If that's okay with you."

"Certainly.

* * *

Marianna surveyed the table. It was a picnic table, and she'd secured the tablecloth with clothespins, but it was a white linen cloth, and she'd used her grandmother's silver cutlery, crystal stemware, and heavy dishes with gold edging. She still did not consider the elegant pieces her own. She was cheating by using the barbeque instead of building a fire pit, but maybe she would try that next year. Everything else was as beautiful as she had imagined it would be.

Dylan had agreed the table looked better set up with the

campground's namesake rock as part of the background instead of right next to the table, though she wondered if he just did not want to move it again. He was right that the flat rock that formed much of the upper part of the beach was more level. Once the table was in place, he had happily and effortlessly carried all the bins to the beach as she had set the table and started the food, without questioning anything or even bothering her with chatter. She suspected he was trying to impress her with strength and sensitivity, and it was working. She looked forward to paying him more attention later. Meanwhile, her guests were coming down the beach stairs right on time.

Sheila gasped in delight as she saw the table. "This is gorgeous." She used her phone to take pictures of the dishes and place settings, then stepped back to take a picture of the table with the ocean in the background. Dylan and Barry greeted each other, and Marianna realized no introductions were necessary. Sheila walked around to the other side of the table to take a few pictures with the Sandcastle Rock in the background and asked Dylan and Marianna to stand on either side of it, then pose in front of it.

Marianna leaned over to Dylan as Sheila adjusted settings on her phone. "Thanks again for trying the table here. She seems to like it."

After several more poses, Sheila announced she was done for now.

"Thank you, Marianna. This is very elegant for a meal on the beach," said Barry.

"It's a special occasion," said Marianna, "and a chance for my grandmother's dishes to get out of the cupboards. Dylan, could you pour the wine, please?" He reached for a bottle nestled into the sand at the edge of the rock and showed it to Barry and Sheila.

"Excellent choice," said Barry.

"Delighted you like it," said Marianna, pleased with his unusual lack of criticism.

Marianna handed Dylan a corkscrew, being sure to brush his hand as he took it from her. She'd avoided any overt flirting earlier, when they were alone, but with dinner underway it seemed appropriate to start. He did not respond to her touch. He opened the wine and poured each glass two-thirds full, the ladies first. Sheila took a picture of him pouring, with the ocean sunset in the background. Marianna offered a toast.

"To Barry and Sheila. Congratulations on your wedding and thank you for allowing us to take part in your matrimonial happiness. As they say in Gaelic, *Mìle fàilte dhuit le d'bhréid, Fad do ré gun robh thu slàn. Móran làithean dhuit is sìth, Le d'mhaitheas is le d'nì bhi fàs.* A thousand welcomes, may you always be healthy, and may you have long, peaceful, and blessed lives." Everyone brushed glasses. Dylan touched Marianna's glass last, and his eyes lingered. She was being appraised. He was interested, but there was something else there.

"Everyone take your seats, please. Cerebus, you too. Sit." The dog walked away from the picnic table, circled a few times, and lay down, stretched out on the warm sand. "He's well trained," said Dylan.

"Airedoodles are very smart," said Sheila.

"I thought you didn't like dogs," said Barry.

"I don't, but it's easy to see Marianna's done a good job training him."

Very smooth, thought Marianna, as she opened the barbeque. She lifted out four large tinfoil packages and set them on a platter. Then she went around the table, placing a package on each plate.

"Oh, a delightful contrast between elegance and casual dining," said Sheila. She snapped pictures of the foil package on the antique porcelain.

"Now open the foils. Mind the steam," said Marianna, "and enjoy."

* * *

Dylan opened his foil packet and admired the contents. There was a whole small lobster, mussels and clams, mini potatoes, two half cobs of corn, an onion, and some greens. Everyone watched as Marianna pulled out the foil to transfer the food to her plate, and they did the same. Marianna gathered the foils, crumpled them into a ball, and threw it for Cerebus.

"Won't he eat it?" asked Barry.

"No. He'll bat it around for a while, then bury it somewhere. It keeps him away from the table. The green stuff is seaweed. Edible, but just leave it if you don't want it."

Sheila took several pictures of her meal, rearranging the food between shots. "This looks amazing. I'm sure it will impress my followers."

"You should stop taking pictures and taste it," said Barry. "Delicious. And you can't get more Nova Scotian than this."

"A fabulous meal," agreed Dylan. He watched Sheila take another picture. The advertising value of Marianna's dinner far outweighed the cost of the food. There had been a note on her website that extras such as a beach lobster dinner were available for purchase, but he had not understood how elaborate it would be. She was as dedicated to her career as he was to his. He also realized he was invited as a prop, to make the dinner more special for the couple, but he would not begrudge them their happiness. And, at the risk of being too vain, he suspected she was flirting with him. Friendly was good, since he'd been abrupt earlier, but if the flirting continued, he'd have to make it clear that he was not interested in a relationship, or whatever she was offering.

As the pile of shells in the centre of the table grew, Barry and Sheila related the story of how they met. Sheila worked for a marketing company, and a project had her eating lunch or dinner at various hotels in Ottawa. Barry installed and repaired hotel computer networks, including business workstations. For several months, their paths crossed, until he accused her of sabotaging equipment to see him again, which she confessed was true. Dylan thought the story sweet, but Marianna seemed less interested. Perhaps she had heard it before.

Marianna cleared the table, and supplied damp cloths, warm from the barbeque, for cleaning hands. "Delicious, but messy," she said.

"Warm cloths to wash with are the thoughtful touches that I love to showcase in my reviews," said Barry.

There was a dessert, blueberry crumble, by candlelight and moonlight. Marianna produced blankets to keep everyone warm as the night deepened, and they lingered over a second or third glass of wine. Marianna reminded Sheila that the wine was from Nova Scotia's own Annapolis Valley, Sheila posed a picture of the bottle behind her glass, catching the fire in the glass, and Dylan admired Marianna's mix of gracious hosting and local promotion.

"I hate to bring such a lovely evening to an end," said Sheila, "but I've finished my wine, and can't handle another glass. I should get to bed before Barry needs to carry me up to the tent."

"Which I would happily do," Barry replied, finishing his wine, and standing up beside her. "Can we carry a few things up?"

"That's not necessary," said Dylan. "Enjoy your honeymoon. We've got this."

"Thanks again for such a lovely evening. It's been perfect. I'll be putting that in my review—ended with a fabulous dinner." They walked up the stairs, holding hands. Dylan tried to understand the look on Marianna's face as she watched them go. Relief the dinner was over and had gone well? Envy of their relationship? Then she looked at him. Was she annoyed he had said we've got this? Or pleased?

At the top of the stairs, they waved and disappeared from view. Marianna let out a breath.

"Congratulations on the great dinner. And it looks like you impressed those social media mavens."

"That's the first time they haven't complained about anything."

"Congratulations, though there was nothing to complain about. I hope you don't mind me saying they didn't need to help."

"Not at all, though I trust you remember you were going to help carry things back?"

"Of course."

She started packing away the dishes. Dylan admired the efficient way Marianna stacked things into the totes, protecting the glasses with the cloth napkins. He made two trips to the house, leaving the totes on the deck where he had picked them up earlier. On the third trip she came with him, carrying a tote herself. Cerebus followed her into the house. Dylan brought the barbeque back up to the deck, then returned to the beach for the last load. He paused at the cleared picnic table, listening to the waves lapping on the beach while looking up at the stars. In Toronto you could not see them. He'd forgotten how many there were.

He brought the last tote to the deck. She'd taken the others inside, and he hesitated, wondering if he should come in or leave it on the deck. The porch door was open, but the inner door was closed. Through the window, he could see Marianna at the sink. He put the tote down and knocked.

She dashed to the door. "Sorry. It's unlocked, just closed to keep the bugs out. Come in, please. Bring that one right to the sink if you don't mind." Dylan walked into the kitchen, following her to the sink.

"Wow! This is gorgeous." The kitchen occupied the back half of the house, with a series of windows facing the ocean, above a long counter. The pink cupboards between the windows and below the speckled counter looked decades old but gleamed as if they'd been painted yesterday. A modern stainless-steel fridge and stove along the far wall contrasted with a huge antique wood-burning stove opposite the windows. "Do you use that?" he asked, pointing at the wood stove.

"Sometimes. If the power goes out, and it's a good source of heat in the winter." Dylan placed the tote on the floor beside her. "Can I help?"

"That's not part of the help I needed, but I will not turn

down help washing dishes. Since I know where everything goes, could you wash?"

Dylan nodded and took her place at the double sink. He could see whitecaps on the ocean through the window, as well as a reflection of Marianna. She grabbed a towel from the oven door handle and started drying and putting away the crystal wine glasses. Dylan added some hot water to the wash tub. "What was wrong with the water earlier?"

"My arsenic filter clogged. I replaced it, but they are expensive. I need to add a cheaper particle filter before it, to help it last longer."

"There's arsenic in the water?" Dylan looked at the rinsing tub, expecting cloudy or tinted water. It was clear.

"Not after my filtration systems. The water here is better than what you get in Toronto. Fresh off the mountain, and triple filtered. I sound like a beer commercial." Marianna laughed.

Dylan cleaned the last glass and added plates to the sink. "You seem to have marketing in your blood. Your dinner was a great promotion."

"Thanks. I learned something at university."

"You went to university?"

"There's no need to sound so surprised. They allow women to attend now."

"Sorry, I just assumed since you were running a campground–."

"That I was uneducated?"

"No, it just doesn't seem like the best career option for a bright young woman." Dylan congratulated himself on a smooth recovery.

"I think you might have been trying to compliment me, so thanks, I guess. Some people want more from life than an office career, a fancy downtown condo, and all that," said Marianna.

"Like I have." Dylan wondered if he was being mocked or teased, but her look and explanation suggested she was teasing him.

"I had the office job and was heading for the condo," said Marianna. "Even looked at a few. Then decided I did not want it. Can you fill this with water for Cerebus?" She handed him a large stainless-steel bowl. "Tepid. Mostly cold, with a little bit of hot at the end."

"I went to university, too. I know the word tepid."

"Oh, so you are more than just a pretty face?" She patted his arm. Definitely flirting, thought Dylan. But he could not resist responding in kind. "I'm touched you noticed. Very astute."

"Yes." For a few minutes, the only sounds were waves through an open window and the gentle clatter of dishes being washed and put away. Then a low rumble started.

"What's that?" asked Dylan.

"Cerebus snoring." Marianna pointed at the dog, sleeping in a corner of the kitchen.

"How did he get that name?"

"I was going through a teen goth phase when I got him, and I figured the name would annoy my mother. That backfired. She thought it was appropriate. She said he chewed so many things in the house it was as if he had three heads."

"You've had him a long time, then." Dylan realized, too late, he had suggested Marianna was old, but she either did not notice, or let it slide.

"Yes. He's an old dog now, but good company. Keeps the coyotes and perverts away."

"You're joking, I hope."

"We'll, I've never seen a coyote here, but they are in the area. And the only reason I can allow a strange man in my kitchen is because if you did anything untoward, Cerebus would defend me. No offense."

"None taken. He doesn't look much like an attack dog, though."

"An Airedoodle is part Airedale and part Poodle. He's loyal and intelligent. And strong. A good combination, in a dog." Marianna looked at him and smiled. She patted his arm again and let her hand linger. Dylan realized she was standing much closer than she needed to. He looked down at her. She smiled up at him, moved closer as if to kiss him, then giggled and crossed to a cupboard, to put away another plate.

Dylan concentrated on not dropping the plate he was washing. She almost kissed me, he thought. He could not be imagining it. Two glasses of wine, with dinner, over three hours—his head should be clear. He placed the clean plate in the rack and started wiping the next one.

She was an interesting woman, and she aroused his curiosity. She had left a good life in Toronto for a small, second-rate campground in the middle of nowhere. Was the Gaelic and the red hair genuine, or an act for the tourists? There was one way he could find out about the hair, he thought, and admitted it was not just his curiosity that was aroused. But a relationship was out of the question, especially now, especially with her, and regardless, he did not know her well enough to consider that. As for one-night stands, Dylan had tried that twice, several years ago. He had no interest in repeating the experience. Maybe she had a different opinion, but he'd have to let her know he was not interested. And without hurting her feelings. Not that her feelings mattered in the long run, but for now he needed more information from her, and wanted to stay on friendly terms.

4

~

Chapter 4

Marianna sat at her desk, waiting for the slow internet connection to retrieve email. Dylan had seemed interested. She'd noticed his pupils enlarging as he spoke to her in the kitchen, and she'd caught him checking her out more than once, his eyes wandering over her body. She'd had a few good looks herself. But after the dishes were done, he had turned down an invitation to stay for a drink, claiming fatigue. She reminded him that Wi-Fi was only available by the house and added that it might be slow if he was planning to video chat with a sweetheart back in Toronto. It worked. He mentioned that he'd broken up with his girlfriend. Before she could offer sympathy, he added that it had been almost a year ago. So, he was straight and single, though if he wasn't over someone from a year ago, maybe she'd be wise to keep her distance.

The computer beeped, an unhappy tone alerting her to a send/receive error. The internet connection seemed okay. She tried again and went to brush her teeth while waiting. Heading back to the computer, she stopped to look out the window. Dylan's tent was dark. "Should we do a little searching," she asked Cerebus, "and see if we can find out more about Dylan?" The dog looked up from his bed in the corner, yawned, and settled down again.

"I'd take that as a yes, but the internet is lousy tonight." The send/receive failed again. "We'll check him out tomorrow."

* * *

Dylan could not sleep. He considered going for a walk, but a glance out the tent flap let him see a light on upstairs at the house. It was absurd, but he did not want her seeing that he could not sleep. She already knew too much about him, and he had learned little about her. Except that she was smart, hard-working, and attractive, and the latter did not have anything to do with her ability to fight the loan cancellation. He picked up his book, read a few pages, and put it down again. Weren't books sold in airport bookstores supposed to be light and entertaining reading? The third chapter had nothing to do with the bank robbery in chapter one, or the sex scene in chapter two. It introduced a family with small children, going on a picnic in a park. There was far too much description of the wicker basket and melamine plates.

Dylan's family had never gone on a formal picnic, but they'd had dinner on the beach several times most summers. It was fun, though less fancy than tonight's dinner had been. The plates had been paper, not melamine or fine china. His dad and some neighbours would build a bonfire, and everyone would roast hot dogs over the flames. He wondered if his sister took her children to dinners on the beach.

He hadn't bothered telling his sister he would be in Nova

Scotia. There did not seem to be any point. She still lived on the south shore, five hours out of the way. They weren't close. He'd never seen her kids or met her partner. They all signed the dollar store cards they sent for his birthday and Christmas, but for the money he sent every holiday, that was the least they could do.

Wondering about beach dinners gave him the urge to let his sister know he was in the province. He picked up his phone and checked the time. Too late to call. A text might have an alert tone, unless she silenced them, but he did not want to risk that. He could use data, and connect to email, but the cell service, at least in his tent, was weak. He'd call in the morning or use the campground Wi-Fi then.

A gust of wind pushed in the side of the tent. The poles sagged and rebounded. Hope it doesn't rain, he thought.

5

Chapter 5

Marianna put down the hammer, wiped sweat from her brow, then realized her hand was black with grime and she'd probably left a dark streak across her face. She'd need a shower after this anyway. It was muggy, and the clouds were heavy. The forecast was for significant rain starting this afternoon. Forecasts, from the Sydney or Port Hawkesbury airports, were rarely accurate for the north end of Cape Breton Island, but this one seemed likely.

Mike and his boys had put in the posts, beams, and trusses for the picnic shelter addition. They had also shingled the roof. They appreciated the early spring work, and her willingness to pay cash, but Marianna planned to complete the walls herself. She liked the physical work and doing some construction herself saved money. Susan, at the Co-op, had suggested Mike, her cousin, for any construction Marianna needed. Marianna had been worried completing the work herself would offend Mike, but Susan assured her he was okay with it, and everyone understood needing to save money.

The side of the bathroom building, and another full wall on the west side, would provide shelter and shade, while half-walls on the east side and facing the ocean would provide natural light, fresh air, and views. She'd almost finished framing the west wall and was adding horizontal braces. It was tedious, without the satisfaction of seeing significant progress. She picked up another short length of two-by-four from the stack she'd cut a few days ago and started nailing the wood into place between the studs.

The hammering echoed across the almost empty campground. Sheila and Barry had left two hours ago, exchanging goodbye hugs with her and Cerebus. Marianna hadn't seen Dylan this morning, and it was almost ten, but he was probably sleeping in. She resisted the urge to check on him. His tent was close to the ocean, where the noise of the wind-driven surf obscured the hammering. Last summer, at a campground on the south shore, an elderly camper had been found dead in his tent. Marianna hoped she would never have to deal with that. But ten wasn't that late, and finding Dylan naked and half out of his sleeping bag would be worse than finding him dead. She swung the hammer harder. Where had that thought come from? She drove the fourth and final nail with just five hits.

Marianna's arm was aching, but there were just two sections left, so she pushed through the ache to complete the wall. The last piece needed to be toe-nailed into the stud. On her first attempt, she bent the nail, but the second attempt worked well. She put the hammer on the concrete floor and stepped back to admire her work. Someone mumbled beside her.

She turned and saw Dylan. His hair was dishevelled, and though he'd looked clean-shaven last night, his stubble was thick this morning. He looked far more rugged than the preppy gym rat who had checked in yesterday, or the polished gentleman who had assisted with dinner. Perhaps the difference in light, she thought. No bags under the eyes though. He'd slept well, despite the suspected lack of camping experience. She hadn't looked him up online this morning, wanting to get work done on the shelter before the rain started. He mumbled something again, and Marianna remembered the ear plugs. She removed them. "Sorry. Not sure what you said, but good morning."

"I said, the wall looks great."

"Thanks. Since the space will be open, I won't finish it on the inside, so this will be visible."

"Makes sense. Hate to be anti social, but I uh, just got up, so I'll come back and chat more in a moment."

Marianna grinned. "Of course." She picked up the hammer, and put it away in the shelter storage room, while Dylan slipped into a bathroom. He was back sooner than expected and greeted her from the other side of the open wall.

"Hello again, and good morning."

"Good morning. Sleep well?"

"Eventually, yes. What are you building here?

"A shelter. I guess that's obvious. My target market is tent campers, and this will be a place to eat or just hang out if it's raining. There'll be sinks and counters along this wall," she said, indicating the back of the bathroom building, "and the rest will be open. There'll be picnic tables, but they can be pushed aside for dancing—I hope to get musicians in, and maybe have ceilidhs some nights."

"Great idea. And you're building all this yourself?"

"I hired guys to do the frame, but I'll do the rest. Plumbing and wiring too, though I'm only connecting to the lines in the bathroom building."

"Wow. That's not part of a marketing degree. Good for you." She looked to see if he was teasing her, but he seemed genuinely impressed. "You have a lot of lumber." He waved at the carefully stacked two-by-fours and sheets of chipboard that took up most of the floor in the shelter.

"That's not just for the shelter. I'm building some cabins, too. No water or power, just something larger and sturdier than a tent. The same time I got this pad poured, I got pads poured to build cabins. Then when I bought the lumber, I bought enough to do the cabins too. If I don't build them this fall, I'll do it in the spring. Doing the concrete and the lumber for the shelter and the cabins at the same time cost more up front but was cheaper than getting two pours and two loads delivered."

Dylan nodded. "Makes a lot of sense. And planning for rain is wise. Looks like rain is on its way. I may hang out under this roof this afternoon. But wouldn't you make more money catering to RV campers instead of tenters? You can charge them a lot more."

"Per night, yes, but according to my research they would not stay as long. Also, there aren't many campgrounds that cater primarily to tent campers, and rising gas prices are cutting into RV sales." Marianna saw open admiration in Dylan's eyes. She'd done her homework, but both her mother and Troy had dismissed her plans as foolish. Drops of water darkened Dylan's light shirt. "You'd better come out of the rain."

Dylan laughed. "I have to shower anyway. I'll get my stuff,

and then maybe settle in here after to do some reading. Unless I'll be in the way of you working."

"No, I'm done for the day." She noticed him looking at her, and realized she was rubbing her sore shoulder.

"Sore?"

"Just a little." She waited a moment to see if he would offer to massage her.

"You should put some ice on it. A bag of frozen peas would be great. Take it easy." He turned and walked towards his tent.

Marianna watched him go, untroubled by the increasing frequency of rain drops. She rotated her shoulder. A massage would be nicer than a bag of frozen peas, but that would have to do.

* * *

The rain shower passed, but the skies did not clear. Dylan ran around the perimeter of the campground, down to the beach, and up and down the shore. On the large flat stony area near the bottom of the stairs he did sets of sit-ups, push-ups, and other exercises, and stretched against the Sandcastle Rock. Climbing back up the stairs from the beach, he thought he saw Marianna at the kitchen window, but she turned away. Had she been watching him? The rain started again. He took his bathroom gear, a change of clothes, and his book to the shelter, shaved and showered, and settled down to read.

Marianna had left a note on a table in the shelter. "There are books at the house, in case you need more to read." The time to read was a luxury, but the book was not holding his interest. He'd try one more chapter, then head to the house, check the selection, and contact his sister. He read a few lines, then a gust of wind blew rain through the unfinished wall. A few drops landed on the book. Maybe I should read in the truck, he thought. He slipped the book into his bag and looked down the hill to the wind-driven whitecaps. It was a shame all her work would go to waste. Unless they kept the building.

Dylan was not sure what the plans for the property were. The client was a foreign company, and he guessed the project would be a resort, if it ever got built. The land alone might be enough for the money laundering, or tax evasion, or whatever the goal was. Dylan was happier not knowing the details. Over the last three years he'd learned his employer made a lot of money from questionable deals. The loans were profitable, but the real money was in failed or cancelled loans and the subsequent seizures or lawsuits. Only the greediest, or naïve, would agree to the terms, so Dylan believed no real harm was done. Marianna was not greedy, but perhaps naïve. He wondered how she compared to other clients. She was the first he'd seen for more than a ten- or fifteen-minute meeting. For most loans, the company gambled on whether the client would pay or fold, but this deal was large and complex, and his bosses wanted to know what she would do. Dylan had been reluctant when asked to come out and spy on her, but he was reminded that it was an order, not a request, and that he'd be rewarded with a large bonus when the client got the land. With his savings, it would be enough to start his own company, and get out of these shady deals.

The rain slowed, and Dylan made a dash for his SUV. Once in, he started the engine and ran it for a few minutes, charging his phone and warming the interior. I should sleep in here tonight, he thought. Cell service was available, but still weak.

He considered walking over to the office, to see if the service was better there, or use Wi-Fi, but the rain continued steadily. He drove over instead, parking in front of the house. The cell signal was stronger here, so he dialed his sister. She rarely answered her phone, and he got the recording he expected. He left a message.

"Hi Jennifer. It's Dylan. Just thought I'd let you know that I'm in Nova Scotia, up on Cape Breton, for work. I don't think I'll be able to make it down your way but thought I should at least let you know I'm here, sort of. Trust all is well with Alison and Cole. Hi to Tina."

He ended the call and caught a whiff of something electrical burning. Smoke was coming from the end of the charging cable. He pulled it out of the console. It was hot to the touch. He'd need to pick up another cord. They were easy enough to buy anywhere. The phone showed 87 percent charge, so it was not a rush.

He connected to Wi-Fi and waited while the phone reacted to notifications from different services. An email from Carla, his manager, asked for an update on his observations. He drafted a response.

Client is overextended and does not appear to have a steady income. Have NOT confirmed she will fold yet. Sorry to be short. Phone and power problems out here in the boonies.

Marianna was tough, smart, hardworking, and resourceful. She might be overextended, and naïve, but she would not give up easily. She might have family members who could help her out. He would find that out today. And she was something to look at too—graceful even when swinging a hammer. Maybe he could learn something that made her less attractive, and more deserving of being wiped out. Dylan decided to drive into the village. He could visit the Co-op store for a USB cable and ask a few questions about Marianna.

6

Chapter 6

"Yes, it's still raining. It won't stop anytime soon, so you might as well go. Come on. Out!" Marianna, holding the door open, waved again to encourage Cerebus to go outside. He stepped past, glaring at her, as if the rain were her fault. She waited at the open door, knowing he would be in the rain for as little time as possible. Dylan still was not back. He'd driven away earlier in the day, and she wondered if he'd gone down the trail to find a motel. Camping in the rain was unpleasant for the most experienced tent campers, which he was not. The wind had flattened his cheap tent, and she could only see it by knowing where to look. The cheap tent did not make sense. After dinner she'd look him up online.

Cerebus brushed against her as he rushed back inside, heading for his bed in the kitchen. She started to close the door, then saw a flash of headlights at the entrance to the campground. She waited as the vehicle came closer, confirming it was Dylan's truck, before closing the door. His return unleashed a flood of emotions, none of which made sense. She was relieved and pleased he'd come back, worried it was to pick up his things and leave, possibly without saying goodbye, and annoyed to be thinking these things. She reminded herself that he'd paid in advance, and that was all that mattered. Then she wondered where he had gone. You wouldn't go out to see the colours in this weather, but wherever he had gone, it probably included dinner. You could hardly cook outdoors in this weather.

She closed the door from the porch and cleaned up the dishes from her dinner. Gusts of wind slammed water against the windows facing the ocean. She didn't hear the knock at first, but was alerted by Cerebus growling, then getting up to bark at the porch door. She opened it and saw and heard Dylan at the outside door. Probably checking out, she thought.

She opened the door, admitting him and a blast of wind and rain. His cheap plastic poncho, smelling new, continued dripping water after he closed the door behind him.

"Thanks. Sorry, I'm getting water all over your floor."

"It's just the porch. That's what it's for."

"Sorry to bother you, but I need to charge my phone. I'm wondering if you have a cord I can use. My car charger died, I don't have another cord to use a USB outlet, and I tried to buy one in the village, but they didn't have any cables made in the last ten years. At least I got some rain gear."

"What's the connection on your phone?"

Dylan extracted his phone from under his poncho and handed it to Marianna.

"Same as mine." She walked into the kitchen. Her phone was on the counter next to the door. She unplugged her phone and plugged his in. "That works."

"Thanks. I'll come back in a few hours, if that's not too late?"

Marianna weighed a quiet evening against learning more about Dylan and being a good host. "It probably won't take long. Sit down, have some tea. Spend a little time out of the rain."

"If you're sure I'm not disturbing you."

"Come in. Hang your poncho here." Marianna grabbed a towel from a shelf over the hooks and passed it to him. "You can dry your face with this."

"Good idea to have that handy." He ran it through his hair.

"Thanks. I keep towels here for Cerebus." He held the towel at arm's length and studied it. "That's a new clean one."

"Hope he doesn't mind using it after me." He finished drying himself. "Where should I put this?"

"Any hook." She stepped back into the kitchen. He took off his soaked shoes and followed her, keeping his distance from Cerebus, who kept trying to sniff him.

"I was just going to make a pot of tea for myself, so it's no trouble." Marianna crossed the kitchen to the stove. "What kind of tea do you like? I'm making herbal for me, but it's no trouble to make another pot. Please, take a seat at the table. Cerebus, leave him alone. He was here last night." Dylan seemed scared of the dog. "He just wants a pet."

"Okay." Dylan gave Cerebus two quick brushes on the top of his head. "I don't like dogs. I guess he can tell. They probably smell it, like fear." But the two pets were enough to satisfy Cerebus. He walked back to his bed, nails clicking on the linoleum floor.

"I don't know about that—he's just being friendly. No reason you can't be friendly back. So, what kind of tea?"

"Just regular tea, with lots of sugar. Thanks." Dylan walked over to the table but remained standing. "Does it often rain like this?"

"No. Heavy rain usually passes quickly. Lighter rain can last for days, though." She set two mugs on the table, spoons, a tea strainer, and a sugar bowl. She extracted four homemade ginger cookies from a large porcelain cookie jar on the counter, set them on a plate, and put that on the table. The kettle started to whistle. She poured the hot water into two small teapots, one brown and one blue, and set them on the table. "Please sit."

She placed the strainer over his mug, then poured the tea from the blue pot. A few leaves caught in the strainer. Dylan sat down, staring at the pouring.

"You've never seen loose tea before?"

"No. I've always used bags."

"This is cheaper, and you can mix flavours if you like. I didn't," she added. "This is plain orange pekoe, like you requested." He wrapped a hand around the mug. Large hands, she thought, but that doesn't mean anything.

"Ah. Nice and warm." He added three spoonfuls of sugar. "This kind of weather can't be good for business."

"It doesn't happen often, especially in the summer. By next season I'll have that shelter finished, so that will be available. I hoped to have it ready this year, but there is a lot of work and expenses to get a campground going."

"You said it was your grandmother's property?"

"It was, so I own the land, but I had to borrow against the land for updating the house, building the bathrooms, upgrading the well and hydro, and so on. But I'm sure we can chat about more interesting things than my work."

Marianna was sure he'd been watching her closely while she got the tea, but now he seemed to be avoiding her eyes. Nervous? "You must have had dinner while you were out?"

He nodded.

"If you don't mind, where did you go, and what did you think of it?" asked Marianna. "I like to keep track of places to recommend."

"Some fish and chip place in Neil's Harbour. I don't remember the name, but it was good. Better than I expected."

"That would be Annie's place. There is only one fish and chip place in Neil's Harbour. Most people like it. Thanks." From the outside, it looked rundown, but the food was good. He'd probably approached it with a big city attitude, another sign that he did not travel as much as he suggested. "Yesterday you mentioned you'd been exploring the east coast. Where else have you been besides here and Antigonish?" She noticed him react, then try to hide it, when she pronounced the town name correctly.

"I've been around the Gaspé Peninsula in Quebec." The lights flickered and went out. The fridge stopped humming, and the rain was louder in the darkness. "So much for my phone charging."

Lightning flashed in the distance, but Marianna didn't hear answering thunder. "It's usually not out long."

"Like the heavy rain doesn't last long?"

Marianna turned away from the window. Dylan was grinning. "Yes. Really."

There was pillar candle on the table. Marianna lit it from a book of matches beside it. "This isn't unusual in bad weather. I have a generator if it's out for a long time." She was tempted to add that the candlelight made the setting more romantic but kept that thought to herself.

"So, you went around the Gaspé? By yourself?" Marianna was wondering about the ex-girlfriend. You could learn a lot about someone by how they spoke of their exes, and whether they were in touch.

"Yvonne, my ex, was supposed to come with me. I had been working to finish my CPA, so we didn't spend much time together. Then I didn't see her at all preparing for the final exam. When I completed it, I'd arranged for a week off so I could travel with her and make up for being so busy." He sipped his tea. "It was meant to be a surprise, but when I told her, she said it was too late, and she was seeing someone else."

"I was cheated on, so I know that's rough. I guess I'm still angry with him. Cookie?" She passed the plate to Dylan. He took one and took a bite.

"Thanks. She didn't really cheat on me. I was angry at first, and I went on the trip partly to spite her. After a few days I realized it was my fault. We'd been together for years, but I'd been so focused on work and school, I took her for granted. So, she found someone who didn't, and who was willing to invest in a relationship. When I got back, I apologized, and wished her well. She's married now, blogs about her pregnancy."

Dylan's attitude and willingness to learn from the relationship impressed Marianna. So different from Troy.

"And you've chosen work? That seems a little ... lonely."

"I have a career plan. I grew up poor, and I didn't like it. When I was fifteen, I worked out where I wanted to be when

I was thirty. I've refined it over time, and I'm a little ahead of schedule. One last deal, and I'll be set."

"There's more to life than work." Marianna realized, as soon as she spoke the words, that her life had been little more than work since she started the campground. When had she last read a book?

"It's more of a life plan. I was going to get married at twenty-five, but the plan was that a partner would fit in without me making any changes. They would fit my schedule. Yvonne helped me realize that was wrong. I've rescheduled marriage for thirty, when my career is well-established, and I can consider making lifestyle choices."

"You date women and tell them you can't marry until you are thirty?"

Dylan made a sour face. "I don't exactly date."

"Just one-night stands?" Guests at a campground were here today, gone tomorrow, and Marianna had learned to strike while the iron was hot if she was curious. Her bluntness might offend guests but, being on vacation, they chatted more than they might at home.

Dylan gave a nervous laugh. "At the risk of sounding old-fashioned, they don't work for me. I'm traditional. Not traditional in that I want a housewife. My partner should have a career of their own. But I do want a partner, someone to live with. Family is the next stage of my life plan. One-night stands don't contribute to the objective, as they say in the office." He took another cookie. "These are great. You made them?" He stared at his tea, both hands on the mug.

Marianna digested what he'd said. No wonder he looked at her with hungry eyes. But he was too repressed. What would he be like if he let go? She imagined him under her, his hands on her hips, raw passion on his face, eyes closed, swollen lips forming her name.

"Marianna? You okay?"

"Yes. Sorry, tired." The candlelight would hide her blushing. He wasn't interested. Besides, another career-focused man was the last thing she wanted.

* * *

It must be the candlelight, thought Dylan. For a moment, in the candlelight, she had looked contented, even well-pleasured, as if after a long session of lovemaking. But she was tired, and he was imagining things he had no business imagining. He had to focus on this deal. There would be an appropriate time for that pleasure, and with someone more suitable. Meanwhile, he needed to know more about Marianna to finish the deal.

"I've told you a lot about me." Far too much, thought Dylan. He hardly knew her but felt comfortable with her. Perhaps it was something to do with being back in his home province, smelling the salt air. "You mentioned your boyfriend cheated on you."

"Fiancé. Troy was my fiancé. We'd been engaged three years." She looked out the window. Dylan watched the candle's shadows flicker around the tendons of her throat. He lifted the plate of cookies to her. "Thanks." She took one but did not bite. "The worst part was he said I shouldn't care because the woman was an escort, so it was nothing personal." She bit the cookie and continued talking. "No, the worst part was he said he was just being one of the guys. He wanted to look good in their eyes—not mine. Or maybe the worst part was when he said it wasn't the first time he'd cheated. The only difference was that I'd found out, and if I hadn't, everything would have been fine."

The lights came back on, the fridge hummed, and Cerebus jumped up, barking. Marianna stood up, brushing crumbs off her top. "Well. Power's back." Dylan realized he was paying too much attention to her hand sweeping down her chest. He stood up and drank his last mouthful of tea. Marianna turned to Cerebus. "You think the rain might have stopped, and you want out again? Come on." She opened the door to the porch. Cerebus followed her to the outer door. Dylan took the empty plate and his mug to the counter. There was still soapy water in the sink, so he washed the two dishes, then went back to the table. Finding her mug empty, he washed that too. She stayed by the outer door, waiting for Cerebus.

When she came back inside, her face was wet from the rain. She dried herself on a hand towel near the sink. "Still raining," she said from behind the towel. "Thanks for cleaning up." Dylan suspected she was hiding tears. She'd seemed upset at the table, and he'd wanted to say something comforting, but the moment had passed.

"I should get going. Thanks for the tea and cookies." Dylan walked out to the porch.

She stayed at the sink. "Hope your tent stays dry."

"I may end up sleeping in the truck. Sorry about your fiancé. Guy was a real jerk." He waved.

"Thanks. Good night." She waved back. Dylan closed the porch door, donned his poncho and still-wet shoes, and crossed the porch. He opened the outside door. Wind-driven rain assaulted him. Definitely sleeping in the truck, he thought. He ran to his truck and climbed in the back. He stripped down to his underwear, spread his clothes over the backs of the front seats, and started the engine to warm the interior. Folding down the back seat made a reasonable sleeping area, and the higher area over the folded seats worked like a pillow once he added a coat. He congratulated himself for having had the foresight to toss his sleeping bag in the truck that morning. He spread it out and shut the engine off. Rain hammered on the roof. She's going to think I'm a real jerk too, he thought, and wondered why that mattered. And I left my phone in her kitchen. I'll get it in the morning.

7

Chapter 7

Marianna woke early, to the rattle of raining hitting the dormer window in her attic bedroom. She got out of bed and looked out at waves cresting high on the beach. They were only halfway to the embankment, and even the waterfront tent sites were well back from the edge. She scanned the cliff edge and gasped. A small stream was cutting across the campground and draining onto the beach. Marianna dashed into the back bedroom. The stream ran all the way down the hill, bisecting the campground. Near the top of the cleared area there was a drainage ditch, intended to divert runoff away from the campground. It must have failed or overflowed.

Marianna dressed in yesterday's clothes, stopped in the bathroom just long enough to use the toilet, raced downstairs, and went into the porch to get rain gear. Cerebus hesitated when she opened the outside door for him.

"Come on Cere. I need to get out there." The dog headed out and stepped down the deck stairs, one at a time, as if he suspected they were slippery.

Dylan was approaching the house. He was wearing his thin plastic poncho over shorts and a T-shirt, and his bare legs and runners were splattered with mud. He waved when he saw her open the door. "Good morning. Sorry, but I've got bad news."

"If you mean my new creek, I know, thanks."

She pulled on waterproof pants and a slicker and stepped into rubber boots.

Dylan climbed up the stairs to the deck and stood under the porch roof extension. "Can I help?"

"I've got it, thanks. You're a guest here."

"It's bad out there, especially around the washroom building. I'd like to help."

Cerebus came back up the stairs and sat beside Dylan. Marianna beckoned the dog, but he did not budge. "You don't want to come back in?" The dog stayed beside Dylan. "Okay. I think I'm being told to let you help." At least he'd asked. He had not insisted she needed help. "You need proper rain gear. There are slickers and rain pants in that cupboard. See if any of the boots in that bin might fit you." She stepped outside and waved him in.

"Don't wait for me. I'll catch up."

"Thanks." She walked away from the house, surveying the damage. The rain was still pelting, pushed in all directions by the wind. The water flowing across the campground had washed out several flowerbeds, and some larger shrubs near the washrooms had fallen over. As she came closer to the washrooms building, she saw some exposed foundation, and realized that water might soon get under the slab. Cerebus ran into the unfinished shelter, shook off water, and settled under a picnic table. She looked around for Dylan but did not see him. Chickened out, she thought, or can't find anything to fit him.

She retrieved a shovel from the utility closet in the back of the building and started digging a trench to divert water away from the building. The waterlogged ground was easy to dig into, but as the flowing water rushed into the new path, it kept trying to flow towards the building. Another shovel entered the ground beside hers.

One foot at a time, they redirected the water, the work going faster with two people. He followed her lead, silently. There was a curious intimacy in sharing the task, but Marianna refrained from making obvious small talk. She'd said too much about herself last night. She was over Troy, and there was no point in remembering what he had said. Though it was not his words as much as the character they revealed. And how foolish she'd been not to see that earlier. As for Dylan, he'd made it clear he was not interested in anything casual, and she didn't want anything else. Even if she did, starting a relationship with a man from Toronto made no sense. One last scoop of dirt, and water rushed down the new trench, away from the shelter and leaving it out of danger.

"We need to see where this is coming from." Marianna started up the hill, following the stream, and using the shovel as a walking stick. She took five steps, then stopped and turned. Dylan was close behind her. "Sorry. Thanks for your help. I need to see where this is coming from."

"I'll come too."

She considered protesting, but she liked the help. Building the shelter, over time, on sunny days, was one thing, but dealing with a potential flood in a rainstorm was another. Any help was welcome. "Thanks." She continued up the hill. Cerebus barked, from inside the shelter, and she told him to stay, but he braved the rain and ran over to her.

She climbed the hill. The path was muddy, and the rain-slicked grass beside it was no better for walking. She almost lost her footing several times. Dylan offered his hand, but she declined. She could see him struggling to walk in gumboots that did not fit. At the treeline, halfway up her property, the problem was obvious. The drainage ditch weaved around an uneven border of balsam firs, but one had blown over. The branches of a small tree blocked the ditch, and the root cavity provided a path for the ditch water to flow out to the campground. They needed to move the tree and fill the hole.

"Move the tree first?"

"Yes. Cerebus, stay here." She pointed to a less soaked patch of grass below a fir tree.

"He's not allowed to explore here?"

"There might be bears or coyotes in the woods. I wasn't worried when he was younger, but he's slower now. Better that he stays where I can see him."

The tree was easier to move than Marianna expected, though Dylan was pulling too, and they both got muddy up to their knees. It was not just his help that she appreciated, but that he did not take charge, and tell her what to do. He's respectful, she thought. He's a frustrating mix of attractive and annoying qualities. Net attraction should be zero, she reminded herself. And this is not a romantic setting. We're soaking wet and covered with mud. I suppose some guys are into that, she thought, but the women are wearing skimpy bathing suits, not rain gear.

"Now, how are we going to fill this in?" Dylan waved his shovel at the space where the roots had been. "Make a wall of sticks from the branches here? I haven't made rivers in the mud for a long time, but I'm willing to try again."

He's trying to take charge, she thought, relieved to find something annoying about him. But he had said we, at least thinking of them as a team. "That might work, or if we can find a few larger rocks, we could use those. Up here." She walked towards an uncleared area above the ditch and used the shovel to push aside the low brush. Dylan followed, copying her search. In a few minutes, they each found a larger rock and carried them to the breach.

"We will need a lot of rocks," said Dylan.

"No, I've got a better idea. See the building over there?" She pointed across the hill to the well house. "There are bundles of asphalt shingles in there. Spares for the roof. We can use shingles to keep back water and build up dirt behind them." She put down the shovel and started walking to the well house, and Dylan followed. She called Cerebus to follow them.

Inside the well house, she took a minute to enjoy being out of the rain and wind. She wiped the water off her face and pulled down the hood of the slicker. I must look a fright, she thought, and then reminded herself that she did not need to impress Dylan. He came into the well house behind her and pulled down his hood. He hadn't shaved this morning, which would have made him look more rugged if not for the bags under his eyes.

"Where are the shingles?"

"Behind the pressure tank. The blue tank," she added, but Dylan was already walking towards it.

Dylan strode across the room and picked up the heavy bundle as if it weighed nothing. "Is one enough?"

"It should be. How does a city boy like you know which one is the pressure tank?"

"I told you I wasn't born a city boy. Let's go." They went back into the rain and wind.

At the ditch, Marianna placed and held the tiles while Dylan shovelled dirt behind them. The work was faster than digging the trench had been, but muddier. Dylan dropped a shovel load of mud, and when a clump landed on his leg, he brushed it away with an equally muddy hand, leaving a black streak. He looked at her and shrugged. Both of their arms were splashed with mud up to the elbows. She struggled to hold the last tile in place against the rush of water, and Dylan shovelled dirt behind it. The water stopped flowing into the root area and started flowing along the ditch again.

"Victory!" Dylan held out his hand for a high-five, then turned his palm in and looked at the mud. "Like your hands are cleaner."

Marianna looked at her own hands, and high-fived Dylan. "Thanks, but don't jinx it. Nature's in charge here. It's not like the city. Let's add more dirt, while we're up here." They worked for a few minutes, filling in the cavity. Cerebus watched from his sheltered spot.

"Thanks again for your help. Least I can do is offer lunch. How about chicken soup?"

He accepted, and they headed for the house. It's a shame these slickers are so effective, she thought. Otherwise, we'd have to get out of our wet clothes. Not that it makes any difference, she reminded herself.

8

≈

Chapter 8

They had missed breakfast, so, once in the kitchen, Marianna proposed a heartier lunch than her first suggestion: grilled cheese sandwiches with tomato soup. Dylan offered to help, and she put him in charge of the sandwiches. Dylan sliced cheese and tried to remember the last time he'd done more than heat a frozen entrée in the microwave. He liked to cook, but there wasn't time.

"A lot plainer than the lunches you usually eat, I'm sure."

"I told you, I wasn't born with a silver spoon in my mouth. I worked hard to get where I am, and I still work hard." He flipped the sandwiches in the pan. The planning and calculations, testing scenarios, and research he did in the office wasn't physical labour, like building a picnic shelter or digging a ditch, but it was still work. Walking down the hill, he'd felt fine, but now that he was standing at the stove, he felt like he'd done a forty-minute workout, with new muscle exercises introduced. Marianna must be very fit, he thought. She was standing close beside him, opening a jar of pickles. He watched her bicep flex.

Muscular. He imagined her legs would be muscular too. He imagined running his hands up her legs, feeling the muscles under the curves, and distracted himself by focusing on the jar of pickles. No label.

"You made your own pickles?"

"Yes. The cukes are local from Bay St. Lawrence. The tomatoes for the soup were mine, from the summer."

"Wow. I didn't think you could grow tomatoes this far north."

"They're a local variety, even called Scotia. My grandmother did a lot of her own preserving, though she didn't have much choice. I do it partly for fun, and partly to save money."

She was resourceful, and he needed to know how resourceful she would be if she needed money quickly.

"You've mentioned your grandmother a few times. Do you have other family here?

"No."

Dylan waited to hear more, then prompted her. "All your family is in Toronto then."

"No."

Dylan transferred the sandwiches to their plates and ladled soup into the bowls. "You don't like to talk about your family."

"There's not much to tell." Marianna carried her dishes over to the table, and Dylan followed with his. "My dad took off when my mum got pregnant. I don't know anything about him, or his family. Mum doesn't like to talk about him. I'm the only child. My grandfather died before I was born. Grandma said he came from out west, and he didn't like to talk about his past. As for Grandma, she was an orphan in England. Came to Cape Breton to marry Grandpa. Came in at Pier 21 in Halifax, took the train up to Baddeck, and never left the island." She dipped her sandwich in the soup. "Thanks for helping make lunch."

"I'm sorry to hear about your dad." Dylan should have been thrilled that she had no family to help, but he felt sorry for her, and angry at himself for feeling sorry for her. He reminded himself that she had gambled and lost. Lots of new businesses went under, and she should have been prepared for that. She was smart, and attractive, but not his problem. The pickles were delicious.

* * *

"Ancient history." Marianna watched as Dylan took a small bite of the pickle, then a larger one. "You like them?"

"They're great. I've never had fresh pickles before. Not fresh, I mean. Handmade?" He seemed enthusiastic but avoided looking at her.

A gust of wind blew rain against the window, and Marianna shivered despite the warm kitchen and hot soup. Dylan seemed warm enough. Even in his T-shirt and shorts, dipping a grilled cheese in soup, there was an aura of strength about him. In a well-cut suit he would dominate a board meeting. She felt warmer than the soup alone could justify. Stop that, she thought to herself, dipping her sandwich and taking another bite.

"What about your family?" she asked him.

"My parents died a long time ago. Car accident. They went off the road."

"I'm sorry. That's rough."

"They both drank a lot. Their way of coping with poverty,

I guess." Dylan glanced at her, then away. Did he think she was poor? "I've got a sister, older. She lives on the south shore. That's where I was born."

"So, will you visit her while you're in Nova Scotia? Or did you already?"

"We're not close."

Marianna waited, took a bite of her sandwich, then prompted him. "Why not?"

Dylan sighed. "She was ambitious when she was young. Wanted to go to university, travel the world. Then a high school romance got all serious."

"She got pregnant?"

Dylan laughed. "No, she's a lesbian. Came out before she started dating."

"And that's why you're not close?"

Marianna's mother had taken her to Pride parades every year, stressed that love was love, and repeatedly told her daughter that she would be loved no matter who she loved. Marianna suspected her mother might be attempting to come out of the closet herself, and that may have been a factor in her parents' divorce. Not that she'd ever seen her mother express interest in anyone. Marianna had no tolerance for homophobia, and if Dylan was that way, it was another reason to avoid any involvement with him.

"No, not at all. I guess I was surprised, but I supported her. Her best friend, who turned out to be her lover, and partner now, didn't want to leave town. I told Jennifer she'd never be happy in the relationship. We argued." Dylan finished his sandwich. "She gave up all her dreams, never travelled further than Halifax, and is tied up with two kids. Her partner is lazy, the type that will never amount to anything. When Tina, that's her partner, got out of school, she got a job driving a forklift at a lumberyard. She'll probably be doing that for the rest of her life. Jennifer could have done better."

Marianna put her sandwich down so she could point an accusing finger at Dylan. "In the first place, I don't see why you would need to approve of her partner. And in the second place, she's got a respectable and steady job, which is no small achievement. Not out here."

"It's not a job that can support a family."

"Are they in financial trouble?"

"I don't know. I send money at Christmas, which I'm sure they need, and I set up education accounts for the kids, because they'll never be able to afford to send them to university. She sends me a thank-you card, but she never writes anything in it."

"I'm not surprised. It sounds like you treat them like the poor country cousins."

"Well, they are poor. My sister has no idea how important money is."

Marianna was about to respond but took another bite of her sandwich first. Then she said, "Some money is necessary, but there's more to life than money."

"You can't eat good wishes. Just look at this campground." He took a bite, and waved at the empty, soaked campground out the window. "You've got a beautiful location, sure, but no customers, in part because of your distance off the main tourist route. You're good at marketing, but even if you market the hell out of this place, it will be hard to make a go of it. Meanwhile, you're planning to build a picnic shelter when your most profitable customers in are RVs and don't need it—and I know you aren't interested in RVs, but even if the sales are slowing, which may be temporary, their owners have money. I just can't see there being money in the tenting market."

Marianna bristled. "My degree is in marketing, and I used to run sales campaigns for Bell Canada. I did a lot of research before starting this place. I'm going after an underserviced and growing market—tent campers. These are people who travel light, with small carshare cars, by bicycle or electric bicycle, scooters, and so on. Even people like you, here with a rented truck. Soon I'll have cabins for them, and this year I rented tents to some people. They want simpler camping without investing a lot of money, generating a lot of emissions, or putting up with a second-rate site because they are in a tent instead of a fancy RV. I've had some unexpected expenses, but it takes years for a campground to break even. This is a long-term investment, and I'm on track." She was exaggerating about being on track, but he'd gotten under her skin. Just like Troy, assuming he knew better than her on almost any subject.

She took her dishes to the sink. He brought his over and offered to wash. She accepted but stayed at the sink. "Thank you. This is the end of my second year, and I've already had some repeat customers, and bookings for next year. As long as I can meet my loan payments, which I am having no trouble doing, I'll be fine. How do you know about the campground business, anyway? Are you scoping out the place for someone?" Not that anyone would want to buy her out. You could make a living from a campground, in theory, but only if you owned the land and ran it, and the property was not worth much. But there was something odd about him and his reason for being there.

"My company does investment risk analysis for different

businesses, including resort properties. Not campgrounds. Sorry to say this, but they're not valuable—just mom-and-pop operations—but the same basic risk rules apply. You have some real challenges here, and I can see you are working very hard—."

"But as a single woman, I couldn't possibly make it succeed? You've noticed there's no pop here."

"Right. He left you, and you've given up on relationships, let alone getting married."

"I don't think my relationship or marital status is any of your business." Marianna concentrated on drying a plate and considered leaving the room. Or asking him to leave, despite the rain. "But I'm single, by choice, and earning a living from my campground."

"I'm sure that marketing degree and your job experience is coming in handy."

She wondered if he was being sarcastic, but his tone was conciliatory. She put the plate away and walked back to stand beside him. "But not making much money, which is apparently all you care about." Marianna glanced at him, but he was looking out the window.

"No. It's not all I care about. It's just that ...." He turned to face her, and looked vulnerable and shy, instead of confident. He looked down at the counter. "I grew up poor. I know what it's like to go to school on an empty stomach, and then telling the teacher I forgot my lunch. And then having the teacher bring an extra sandwich because I forgot mine so often." He turned back to looking out the window, as if searching for something on the sea, and rested his hands on the countertop. "I wasn't just hungry, I was ashamed. My parents never thought money was important. Dad drank away whatever money he could pick up from odd jobs. Mum made money sewing dresses for women in the neighbourhood, but I think it was just a way for them to give us charity money without anyone feeling awkward. When I was little, maybe four, my grandpa told me he would teach me carpentry, like he did, so I'd have a good job and always enough to eat. Then Grandpa Bill died."

Marianna looked down at the counter, unsure how to respond to Dylan's revelations. Then she put a hand over his closer one. He turned to face her. "It's okay," she said. His stubble made it easier to see a faint scar on his cheek. They were close enough that she could kiss him. She wanted to, and not in the flirting way she had almost kissed him last night. Something deeper was urging her forward. It was not quite lust, and it was more than comforting him. She was already doing that, feeling the heat of his hand under her palm. He's not interested, and this would not be a good idea, she reminded herself. She lifted her hand from his and picked up a bowl to dry.

"Thanks," he said. "Sorry. That was uncalled for. I don't know what brought that on. Being back at the ocean, maybe. The view from my childhood kitchen was like this. Except I don't ever remember it raining like this."

"No need to apologize. Thanks again for helping with the dishes."

"You cooked," said Dylan, "so it's only fair."

"That was to thank you for helping with the flooding," said Marianna.

"Let's call it even after this," said Dylan.

"Deal. No soap in that pan. Just rinse it under the tap." She appreciated the lighter mood.

Dylan turned on the tap, but no water flowed. "Pump not working again?"

Marianna flipped the kitchen light switch, but nothing happened. "The power's out, again."

Dylan patted his pockets. "Right. I left my phone here last night." He walked over to the counter where it was still plugged in. "There's cell service. Good strength." He unplugged the charged phone and put it in his pocket.

"The cell tower is a few kilometres past the gate. So that means it's a wire down along the road, after the tower, and not a big area outage. I'm the only customer affected, so I'll have to check it and call it in." She'd been with Dylan all morning and looked forward to some distance. She could hardly ask him to hang out in his tiny wet tent, or the half-finished shelter.

"Maybe it's a breaker?"

"No. My power splits into two lines at the gate. One goes up to the well house, and the other comes down here. Since neither the pump nor the house have power, it's out on the road, unless both my lines came down. That's unlikely. I don't have trees above the lines here, and there are lots along the road, where it hugs the mountain. Soon after I moved out here, a tree blew down across the road and took out the line. It's probably that again." She opened the kitchen door and stepped into the porch.

"Where are you going?"

"Before I call them, I'll drive down the road and check what the problem is. Saves time if I can tell them whether they need to bring a new pole."

"I'll come with you."

"Not necessary. I'm not some damsel in distress, and you are still my guest. Since I don't have a shelter yet, I sometimes let people hang out in my living room. There are some books in there. Make yourself at home. I'll be back soon." She closed the door without waiting for his reply.

9

∽∾

Chapter 9

Dylan heard the outer door close. Cerebus looked up at Dylan.

"I know," Dylan said to the dog. "She couldn't wait to get away from me. After that scene in the kitchen, I don't blame her. What is it about her?"

Cerebus didn't answer.

Dylan walked past the table down a short hall and into the front room of the house. She wasn't kidding about some books in here, he thought. The wall on the inner side of the room was built-in bookshelves, top to bottom. In front of the bookshelves were two worn couches, with scattered blankets and pillows. The couches faced the outside wall, with built-in shelves around the windows. A TV partially blocked one window, and there was a stack of kid's movies on the DVD player next to it. Board games, children's toys, and more books filled the shelves. Kid friendly place, thought Dylan, once again admiring Marianna's resourcefulness. A woodstove nestled in the front corner, with a stack of wood taking up much of the front wall.

Dylan squeezed behind a couch to look over the bookshelves. Older books along the upper shelves caught his eye. He pulled out a worn book, glanced over the opening pages, hesitated, then turned to chapter one and started reading.

"Find something?"

Dylan turned and saw Marianna in the doorway. "*The Blue Lagoon*. I had no idea it was this old. This book is from 1921."

"Yes, and it's much better than the movie. Most of the books were my grandmother's, except the board books and Golden Books. Those were my mum's when she was little."

"You didn't inherit the love of reading?"

"I did. I think I read *The Blue Lagoon* every summer I visited. Used to love that story. But I also read eBooks, and there's a library in Ingonish. I can get books from any library in Nova Scotia sent there." She paused.

Dylan realized she could not have driven anywhere in the few minutes since she had left. She still had her slicker on. "Car trouble?"

"Yes. My truck won't start. The alternator's been weak for a while, and now the battery is dead."

"I can give it a boost, if you have jumper cables."

"That will start it, but I need to replace the alternator for it to run properly. Can you just give me a ride to check down the road?"

"So, you are a damsel in distress?"

"I guess so. But I don't like it."

Dylan grinned at her pout. "I'll go get my truck."

She followed him out to the porch and offered the loan of rain gear again. "There should be something dry in the cupboard."

"I'm only walking back to my truck, and then I'll crank the heat. This thing will be fine for that." He lifted his plastic poncho off a hook.

"Hang on." She leaned past him and burrowed among the collection of hanging coats. She was not wearing any obvious fragrance, but her earthy scent was a pleasant note above the plastic smell of his new poncho. Dylan noticed her bra was loose enough to let her breasts shift under her shirt as she reached. He looked away and wondered if he should reconsider his opinion of one-night stands. He could not recall being this attracted to a woman he barely knew, but he usually wasn't this close to one, either.

She extracted a large blue fleece kangaroo jacket and offered it to Dylan. "At least put this on under that thing. Keep you warmer." He accepted it and pulled it over his head. It was snug, but comfortable.

"Fits great. You keep extra jackets for guests too?"

"No, but people leave things behind. If I know who it belongs to, I offer to mail it home. If they don't want it, or I don't know who it belongs too, I keep it in case someone needs something."

"A clothing library."

She nodded.

"I'll get the truck and pick you up here." He recalled the inside of the truck being a mess.

"Nonsense. I'll come with you. Be right back," she called to Cerebus, and followed him out the door.

The rain was coming down as heavy as it had all day. The ditch repair had held, but the campground was still soaked, and they took small steps to avoid slipping on the wet grass or muddy driveways. Dylan's tent had collapsed. She stopped to help pick it up, but he kept going, opened the passenger door of his truck, and motioned for her to get in. He offered a hand to help her up.

"My, what a gentleman." She smiled at him but didn't accept his hand, and climbed in. "Let's not take this damsel in distress thing too far. I have a truck myself, though not as fancy as this one." Dylan nodded. Rain was blowing into the truck. He closed her door.

The ground was so wet he raised his flattened tent, stakes and all, with one pull. I'm lucky this didn't blow away, he thought, though it's not doing me much good. He opened the rear glass on the SUV, pushed his sleeping bag to one side, and tossed his tent in. That would ensure he'd still have it tonight, and it might be drier. He walked around to the driver's door, opened it, and saw his bright red underwear hanging from the driver's seat headrest. "Sorry about the mess. I wasn't expecting company." He tossed the still damp briefs onto the back seat, climbed in, and pulled off the dripping plastic poncho and tossed it on the floor behind the seat. He pulled his phone from his pocket and placed it in a cupholder, started the truck, and turned on the heat.

* * *

Once on the road, Marianna reminded him to watch for a downed wire, but the poor visibility from the rain made slow driving necessary on the curving mountain road. Where the road hugged ravines along the face of the mountain, swollen streams threatened to overflow the culverts and flow across the road.

"Maybe it's a good thing I got a four-wheel drive," said Dylan.

Marianna couldn't remember seeing the streams this high, but she only drove to Bay St. Lawrence once every week or two. There were more potholes than she remembered from her last drive in.

"There." Dylan stopped, and she pointed at a hydro pole. Wire ran from the pole towards the campground, but there was no wire on the other side of the pole.

"That's all you need to see?"

"No. We need to continue and see why it's down. Probably a tree. Watch for the other end of the wire. It might be on the road." Around the next corner, the end of the wire was visible, hanging down from a leaning pole. "Keep going," she said. "Something up ahead pulled the wire." Dylan crept ahead while Marianna watched the wire. She realized her chainsaw was still in the cargo box in her truck. If there was a tree down, they'd have to come back to clear the road. She realized they'd have to come back, anyway. The chainsaw was dangerous, and she would not use it in this weather. Dylan would not be able to leave if a tree blocked the road, but he'd have to wait. He hadn't said anything about leaving, but this was not much of a vacation for him. If he was here for a vacation. She reminded herself she needed to look him up or ask some questions.

They drove around another corner. "Oh," said Marianna. Dylan also saw the cause of the problem and stopped the truck.

At a curve over a ravine, there was a gap of about two metres in the road. In the gap, she could see the top of a culvert where the road above it had washed away, taking a power pole with it. Despite the wipers, it was hard to see through the windshield, and she couldn't see anything through the side window. She put her phone on the dash to keep it dry, opened the door, climbed down, and closed the door, trying to keep the leather seat dry. Wires lay across the road on both sides of the gap.

Dylan got out and walked around to her. "Watch out for live wires," he shouted over the rain and wind.

Marianna pointed at the next pole, across the gap. "There's no power after that pole. The wire on this side is not live. But they won't be able to fix the power until the road is fixed." She turned back to the truck and opened the door, struggling against the wind. She reached for her phone. "I'll have to call—." Marianna heard a rumble. It wasn't wind. The ground shook. Dylan grabbed her arm and pulled her away from the truck. "Run!"

They ran behind the truck and up the road, away from the ravine. The rumble grew louder, rattling like waves running through stones on the beach. Small rocks blew past them, some stinging her back. The groaning reminded Marianna of a minor earthquake she'd experienced years earlier in Toronto. Was the ground shaking again or was it just the sound? The noise faded. Marianna and Dylan had reached the previous curve in the road. She realized he was still holding her arm. He let go, and they turned around.

The landslide had washed out a large section of the ravine, pulling down trees. The culvert, and the surrounding road, had been carried away. Trees and the power pole from the other side leaned into the deep cut over rushing water, heard but not seen. The pole pivoted and fell deeper into the hole. The road on both sides started collapsing, and the opening yawned wider.

The opening reached Dylan's SUV. As Marianna watched,

it tilted forward. The road disappeared under the front wheels, and then the truck fell into the gap and it disappeared. Breaking glass and crunching metal added to the roaring wind and rain. Marianna could hear the truck crashing against rock after rock, and saw it come to rest where the ravine reached the sea, over a hundred metres below, upside down and with water splashing over the exposed underside. She looked at Dylan. He was white, expressionless. *Is he in shock? Am I in shock?* She shivered.

"We could have been in that, " he said.

"I know."

Dylan turned to her. "You okay?"

"No," said Marianna. "You?"

"I'm glad we weren't in that."

She wasn't sure if he was joking or stunned. He appeared to shiver, perhaps from the cold. His jacket was soaked and plastered against him. She turned and hugged him, to reassure him and herself.

* * *

Dylan wanted to laugh. It was a nervous reaction, and she'd think he was in shock. Maybe he was, but not because of the truck. That was a rental. All he'd lost was a few clothes, easily replaced, and cheap camping gear he was never going to use again. His shock was from Marianna wrapping herself around him. He was not sure if it was her need for comfort, or her desire to comfort him. Regardless, she held him tight, and he embraced her. Everywhere they touched was warm, which made no sense, since her rain-slicked coat pressing against him soaked him through to the skin anywhere he was not already wet.

Lost my phone, he thought, and laughed. Marianna stepped back. "Are you okay?"

Could I have possibly screwed this up any more than I have, Dylan wondered. "I wanted a vacation," he said. "Now I don't even have my phone. Or any clothes. It's absurd."

"My phone …. It was in the truck, too. I have a shortwave radio back at the house. I can use that to call in the washout. But we need to get back to the house first. Let's go."

"Would it be easier to walk to the village?"

"Even if we could get across this, we are closer to my place than Bay St. Lawrence. Let's go."

She turned and started walking. Dylan stepped up to walk beside her. She'd been shaken, but overcome it, and taken action. She would not quietly accept the loan being called. *What will she do? What will I do?*

10

Chapter 10

I will never go out in the rain without a serious raincoat again, no matter how short a time it is, thought Dylan. He didn't even have the plastic poncho but was grateful for the jacket Marianna insisted he wear, soaked as it was. At least the rain was slowing to a light drizzle. The wind had died down too, though that could be the shelter effect of the trees on either side of the road. Beside him, Marianna opened a few buttons of her raincoat.

"No point in both of us being soaked," he said.

"It's not waterproof anymore. I'm already soaked. No point in being sweaty too."

"It's warmer than I thought it would be."

They skirted a puddle that took up most of the road. Talking would pass the time, thought Dylan. It would take his mind off how wet he was. "Last night, you mentioned your fiancé cheated on you. I never got a chance to sympathize, and it sounds like you got it worse than I did. I'm sorry that happened to you. It sounds like he was a jerk, and you're better off without him, but that was still awful."

"Thanks. I'm over it now."

He waited, but she didn't offer to provide details. Was it too nosy for him to ask? "But you don't want to talk about it."

"No."

They crested a hill and had an open view to the ocean. The wind had died down and the surf was quieter. The road curved into the mountain, leading to the next ravine. Dylan could hear water rushing down it. "I hope there are no more washouts on the way back."

"We worked at the same company. I was in marketing; he was in finance. The company frowned on co-workers dating. It was okay if you were in different departments, which we were, but Troy was very career focused. Like you. He didn't want to risk upsetting anyone, so we kept the relationship secret. He also worked long hours, so we didn't see each other often."

"But actually, he kept things secret and worked long hours to have affairs?"

"Yes. He really did work long hours, most of the time, and was going up the career ladder. He kept telling me we would be public soon, he'd have more time soon, and I tried to be accommodating. I finally gave him an ultimatum, and he proposed. But no ring. He still wanted to keep things secret."

"And then you found out he was cheating." No wonder she flirts with campers, thought Dylan. After years of being accommodating, she wants to be in control.

"Yes. And got those stupid explanations. Along with excuses about how he had to focus on his career, and he was giving our relationship all the time he could spare, but we weren't married yet and he wasn't going to turn down any opportunity for fun, meaningless sex. His words. He said I was being old-fashioned and unreasonable." Marianna stepped to one side to slam her boot into a puddle.

"I don't think you were unreasonable. He was." Troy had been such a slimy character, Dylan wondered what she had ever seen in him. The notion that anyone would mistreat Marianna made no sense to Dylan. That he worried about it startled him.

"Now here's the best part. When I told my mum I was leaving him, she agreed that I was being unreasonable. She told me not to expect perfection from men, be accommodating, and forgive him. Can you believe that? From a woman born in the 1960s? And divorced?"

Dylan considered saying something about the power of forgiveness but kept quiet. His breakup with Yvonne had been about as respectful as these things could be. They were still friends, at least online. She'd suggested going out for coffee once or twice, but it had been easy for him to say he was too busy, and she never pointed out that was why they broke up.

"I'm sorry your mum didn't support you. She sounds old-fashioned herself."

"She is, in a lot of ways, and yet she's progressive in some ways too. I don't understand her, but I suppose children never understand their parents." They crested another hill. "Almost there. The campground is over the next hill. I'm looking forward to dry clothing."

"Me too. Or I would, if I had something to change into."

"Don't worry about that. I have clothes for you."

Dylan glanced at Marianna. She was shapeless in her rain

gear, but he'd seen the curves he knew it was hiding. She also came up to his chin. "I don't think I'll fit your clothes."

"My clothing library, remember? It's not just coats. You'd be surprised what people leave behind. You won't go naked, unless you want to."

Dylan was unsure how to respond to that.

"But I wouldn't recommend it. Mosquitoes."

They walked the last section of road and through the water-logged campground in silence. In the open area, the wind was stronger, and the rain became heavier again.

"Made it," said Marianna, as she held the porch door open for Dylan. "I'm really sorry about everything you lost. Your camping stuff, the rental truck, your phone."

"You could hardly have expected the road would collapse. No one got hurt. Now we need to get out of these wet things and get warm." Dylan thought he saw a grin flash and fade on Marianna's face.

* * *

Marianna stepped out of her boots, took off her raincoat, and hung it on a hook. Everything she wore was soaked through and dripping, and the sensible thing would be to strip in the porch. Dylan, beside her, hung up the dripping kangaroo jacket, pulled off his sodden runners, then turned to look out the porch window. She noted the muscles on his upper back, outlined under the shirt stuck to his skin. Lower down, his shorts stuck to his firm butt, feeding rivulets of water running through the hair on his legs. She looked down at herself. Her shirt clung to her chest and might have been transparent for how visible her bra was.

"We should strip everything off," he said. "You go first. I won't look."

"Sure." She was too cold to disagree. "There are more towels on the shelf, so you can cover yourself with that before you come in. Just throw everything in a pile on the floor. We can squeeze them out over the sink and hang them to dry inside once we are dressed."

Marianna stripped off everything except her panties and dumped the wet clothes in a pile on the floor, then wrapped a towel around herself. She looked up and confirmed he was still looking out the storm-dark window. She caught his eyes in the glass.

"Were you watching my reflection?"

"I swear, not. Just checking the view. Outside. The rain."

"Wait for me in the kitchen. I'll be right back."

Marianna rushed upstairs, startling Cerebus. She peeled off the wet underwear, ran a towel over herself, and dressed. She returned to the kitchen to find Dylan lounging on a kitchen chair, a towel draped around his waist. His wallet was open on the kitchen table, with credit cards and a handful of soaked twenty-dollar bills spread out beside it. His chest was as muscular as she'd imagined, finely patterned with black hair in a T pattern. He noticed her looking at him.

"Only fair," she said, "since you were watching me change."

"I confess to seeing your bra, but only on the floor. I didn't think you were the lacy bra type."

"I hardly think you know me well enough to know my underwear."

"Probably best if things stay that way. But I can remove my

towel if you're feeling shortchanged." He moved his hand to his waist.

"No, that's not necessary. Let's get you dressed. Follow me."

Marianna led Dylan upstairs to the second bedroom. "This is where you will sleep tonight," she said, surprising herself with how firmly she made that announcement. She waved him into the room, looking away, but catching his scent as he passed close to her.

"I put away all the lost-and-found clothes in that dresser. I don't keep underwear, but you could wear swim trunks or shorts for boxers. There are several pairs there."

"Now who's assuming underwear preferences?"

Marianna changed the subject. "I'll get a fire going in the stove to dry the clothes and warm us up."

"Thanks. I feel like I've been upgraded from a tent to a luxury bed and breakfast." He waved at the wallpaper. "*Alice in Wonderland* wallpaper with matching curtains and quilt. Fancy."

"This was my room when I came here in the summers. One year Grandma asked me to help her redo the room, and this what we came up with. Now that I live here, my room is the larger one with the ocean view. I'm not sure what I'm going to do with this room, but you can use it for now."

"Sorry to be such trouble."

"Nonsense. It's the least I can do, now that you are trapped here. I don't know how long it will take to fix the road, but we can get you out by boat as soon as the weather clears."

"What about the bathroom? No water, so, um, is there an outhouse or something?"

"This may not be Toronto, but there are no outhouses here.

The toilet flushes using rainwater collected on the roof. I save money by not needing to pump and treat the water. Unfortunately, I was not allowed to do that for the bathroom building. Anyway, it works just like a regular toilet. Keep the lid closed so that Cerebus doesn't drink out of it. I've got toothbrushes, disposable razors, and so on, at the front counter. I'll bring some up for you." She turned to leave, then stopped at the door and turned back. "Sorry my ride request turned into such a disaster, but thanks. Your company was appreciated."

Marianna turned and raced down the stairs. Why was it nerve-wracking to say thanks to him? Maybe because he was in her house wearing nothing but a towel? He wasn't her first male guest, though the first to have the spare bedroom. Which is where he belongs, she thought. Attractive as he was, there were too many unknowns and red flags for him to be anywhere else.

She lit the fire in the stove, set up an indoor clothes drying rack in front of it, and collected the wet clothes from the porch. He wore sensible Fruit of the Loom briefs. She draped them beside her panties, then decided that was too familiar, and moved them to a separate rack. She combed her wet hair and topped the water for Cerebus.

With the kitchen warming up, she decided she was ready to face the outdoors again. Her generator was under the deck. She'd saved money on the purchase and installation by getting a manual start unit, and not wiring it into the house wiring, but she'd run heavy-duty extension cords from the generator into three rooms, the kitchen, the office, and her bedroom, so she could have power where she needed it once the thing was started. It caught on the third try. She went around the outside of the house to the office entrance. Once inside, she plugged the radio into the generator cord, and tried to reach someone. Mike, at home in Bay St. Lawrence, responded after several attempts. The transmission was garbled. She explained that the road to the campground was washed out, and she'd lost her phone, but she was fine. One guest was stranded, but they agreed it made more sense for him to stay at the campground for now. She went back outside and around the house to shut off the generator and return to the kitchen. Dylan was waiting for her, in baggy sweatpants and a snug fluorescent pink T-shirt with a glittering silver unicorn across his chest.

"I think I know why these clothes get left behind. What can I make for dinner?"

Marianna burst out laughing.

11

Chapter 11

"Glad you find this amusing," said Dylan. He was pleased to make her laugh but did not think he looked that funny. "You've had a rough day. I thought I could help out."

"I'm sorry. The clothes look ridiculous, and you bustling about in my kitchen, in that getup. No. Sweet of you to offer, but I'll get dinner. I've got halibut in the freezer I should use before it thaws. Potatoes and carrots in the cold room. I'll use up the milk to mash the potatoes. You okay with that?"

Dylan nodded. He would not have to figure out cooking on a wood stove. "I'll wash up, then, but what about water? From the cistern and boiled on the stove?"

"Sort of. The cistern is not very big, and only for the toilet. The excess goes to a larger tank in the basement. But yes, we'll boil it on the stove. I've got some bottled water, but I'll save that for now."

Dylan looked around. "I can bring some water up, then."

"There's no need. I have a bucket, but you don't need to get it from the basement." Marianna picked up a bucket hanging from the far side of the stove, walked over to the sink, and lifted drying-up cloths, revealing a hand pump. "This is original to the house. It was connected to a shallow well, but that dried up decades ago. I used to play with it as a kid, but never got any water. Now it's hooked up to the basement rainwater tank." She put the bucket in the sink and started pumping. Water flowed into the bucket.

"Impressive. And you use the old hand pump instead of an electric pump for when the power is out."

"Yes. It's a backup water source. It's also a promise I made to my grandmother." Marianna stopped pumping, but kept a hand on the pump, and looked out the window. "The first visit I remember, I asked her why the pump didn't work. She told me the fairies were mad at her for putting in another well. I told her I would talk to the fairies and fix it, but I couldn't find them. I got so frustrated and upset looking for them that she finally told me there weren't any, and that made me even more upset. Apparently, I told her there were fairies, and I'd prove it by finding them and fixing the pump. On later visits it was a joke between us. By setting up the tank, it's like I made peace between my grandmother and the fairies. You probably think that's silly." She resumed pumping.

"No. It's delightful. Sweet." Dylan thought of his sister, telling him a bedtime story that involved looking in the drawers and the closet for fairies. That seemed a long time ago.

"Why don't you read something while I get dinner?"

"I should help. Besides, the book I was reading got washed away with everything else. Not that I was into it."

"Sorry. You've seen the living room—I'm sure you can find something else to read. And, not to be rude, but I don't like to chat while cooking. I'm used to living alone and I could use some quiet time."

"No need to apologize. I'll leave you alone. But if you can call me ten minutes before it's ready, and show me how to use the stove, I can make a sauce for the fish. I'm sure you have ingredients for a couple possible sauces, but I'll find everything I need without bothering you."

"Deal." Marianna selected some potatoes from a bin in a lower cupboard, put them in the sink, and pumped water to wash them.

Dylan walked out of the kitchen, past the drying clothes beside the warm stove. Seeing his socks hung beside her bra was an oddly familiar sensation. Not déjà vu, he thought, but a glimpse of the future. That makes no sense, he thought. It's not my future, or hers.

In the living room, he scanned the books, glancing at the titles on the spines. Why would he have a thought of a future with her? He hardly knew her, but he'd had a similar sensation when they hugged after his truck fell into the ravine. The excitement of the close call, it must be. What a mess. The lost rental truck, and the camping supplies, all of which he had just purchased, was a minor nuisance, but his job was harder than expected. Not only did he not want to hurt Marianna, but he was also attracted to her. He should leave as soon as possible, whenever that might be. The road was washed out, and the rain was still pounding against the walls and windows of the house. Even if he could leave, that wouldn't solve the problem of her loan.

The end of a top bookshelf contained magazines and calendars, wedged together. They looked decades old. He reached up and tried to pull out a magazine. A bundle fell apart and landed around him on the floor. Among the items was a blank letter-size envelope, the paper yellowed. He picked up the envelope, felt the folded paper inside, took it out, and unfolded it. It was a letter, dated May 17, 1985. He started reading, curiosity overcoming any sense of snooping.

Dear Helen,

As I begin this letter, I remain unsure if I should post it. Although I am your mother, I am not in a position to judge your lifestyle. And I appreciate that you trusted me enough to share the challenges of your arrangement with Russell. But I want to make it clear that I never thought you handled this well, and with his passing, you have a chance to provide a more stable home environment for little Marianna—.

Dylan tore his eyes from the letter. He shouldn't read more. He folded the letter, following the original creases, and tucked it back into the envelope. Marianna had told him her father had left the family, but this letter, presumably from her grandmother to her mother, suggested otherwise. Had Marianna lied to him? Or did she not know? Should he bring it to her attention? But she might think he had read it. The best option might be to put it back exactly where he had found it. But she should know about it, if she did not. He slipped the envelope under a table, placed one magazine on top of it, and replaced the others on the shelf.

The book next to the magazines was a faded paperback, *The Cautious Amorist*. The blurb on the back promised a comic tale of three men stranded on an island with a woman. As the book was a 1947 reprint of a 1932 book, Dylan assumed it was, at most, mildly suggestive. He flipped through the book and noticed writing inside the cover.

"To my dearest Kate. You might enjoy this tale of a clever woman. Love always, E. G. D. Christmas 1997 xo." The book's plot made it an unlikely choice for a romantic gift, unless E. G. D. was familiar with Kate's reading habits. Dylan wondered who the lovers were, and how the book ended up here. Marianna had said most of the books were her grandmother's, but the date was long after her grandfather died. Perhaps it was left behind by a camper. Or perhaps Kate was her grandmother, and she'd had lovers after her husband died. Was that why she couldn't judge Marianna's mother's lifestyle? And what was it? None of this has any bearing on calling in the loan, he reminded himself. There was no need to know more about Marianna than was necessary for that, however fascinating she was.

Dylan put the book back on the shelf. The lost-on-a-desert-island plot reminded Dylan he had read the first chapter of *The Blue Lagoon*. He found it again and settled on the couch.

* * *

Marianna had a spice mixture planned for the fish, but she left it plain for Dylan's sauce. With everything ready except the fish, she stepped into the living room to let him know it was time to make the sauce. "As for the stove, the front ring on the left is basically high, the one on the right is medium." He declined her offer of further assistance. "I'll leave you to it, then."

As he passed her, he apologized for knocking some magazines off a shelf. "I cleaned everything up, but sorry if I missed anything or put them back out of order."

"I've no idea what order the magazines are in, if any. Not to worry, thanks." He nodded and disappeared into the kitchen. She looked over at the indicated stack of magazines. The room seemed no different from usual, until the corner of a magazine, peeking out from under an end table, caught her eye. She bent down, extracted the magazine from its hiding place, and returned it to the shelf. A yellowed envelope remained on the floor.

She opened it and read the letter. She read it twice, start to finish, then read some phrases again. She sat down on the sofa. This was not the loving, kindly grandmother she knew. No wonder Mum rarely speaks of her, she thought. She tried to recall signs of animosity between her mother and her grandmother, but there hadn't been anything more than unexplained distance she assumed was due to her mother settling in Toronto. And the letter had never been mailed. What did her grandmother mean by referring to Marianna's father's passing? Was that a euphemism for him abandoning her and her mother? Her mother never missed a chance to mention how she'd been abandoned, though the details were vague. Marianna had always assumed her mother did not want to talk about it. Her grandmother had never mentioned Marianna's father, and once when Marianna had asked if she knew him, her grandmother said she did not want to talk about him. Marianna wanted to call her mother and ask what the letter meant, but with no phone, no cell service, and no internet service, it would have to wait.

Dylan called from the kitchen. "Everything is ready."

* * *

Marianna watched with satisfaction as Dylan cleaned up the sauce on his plate using the last of the mashed potatoes.

"Dinner was delicious. Thank you."

"Your sauce was a tasty addition, thanks." Marianna got up from the table, but Dylan jumped up and took her plate, added his, and took them to the sink.

"Should it be your turn to read for a while?"

"Perhaps I should. After spending an entire dinner talking about old TV shows, you must think I've never read anything, and just keep the books for show." She'd been happily distracted from her grandmother's letter by the discovery that she and Dylan had had a mutual fondness for *Rugrats* as children, and other shows as teens.

"I watched them too, so I'm not going to judge." Dylan took a pot of steaming water from the stove and poured it into the sink. Marianna watched him, and again she felt that he was entirely too comfortable in her kitchen. She fed Cerebus, then approached the counter beside Dylan. "I'll dry." Third night in a row, she thought. The tight shirt revealed his nipples and every motion of his chest muscles as he scrubbed a fork. A gust of wind pushed water against the window. Marianna looked outside. It appeared to be getting lighter. Maybe the weather was clearing. "It seems rude of me to read while you do the dishes."

"I read while you cooked."

"That's different. Remember, you're my guest, and I prefer not talking while cooking. Besides, you cooked too. How did you learn to make that sauce from scratch? I thought you didn't cook much."

"I don't. But several years ago, I took a cooking class."

"Why?"

"Promise not to laugh?"

Marianna snorted, but his expression made it clear he was being serious. Save me from the male ego, she thought. She forced a grim face. "You didn't laugh when I told you about the fairies. I'll be good."

"I was hoping to meet women."

Marianna bit her lip and turned away.

"That's not the funny part."

"No, I guess not. What happened to not dating?"

"This was before I met Yvonne. Before I really started to focus on work."

"Okay." Thanks for the reminder that you're not available, she thought. "So, what's the funny part?"

"The whole class was guys. I think all of us had joined for the same reason, but none of us would admit it."

Marianna started to snicker.

"Then of course we had to outdo each other. We made dishes as complex as possible. We competed for the hottest sauces, the fastest prep, the sharpest knives. I guess it is kind of funny."

Marianna started laughing. Dylan wiped the last pot clean and placed it in the drying rack. He was about to pull the drain plug when she grabbed his upper arm to stop him.

"Wait—I always wash Cere's bowls too." His forearm was thicker and firmer than she expected.

Dylan looked down at her hand, and she pulled it back. "Sorry."

"I'll get his bowls."

"Thanks."

She waited by the counter as Dylan got the bowls, washed them, and placed them in the rack. He looked at her, she nodded, and he drained the sink. He dried his hands on his pants and looked at her. She stood there with the drying-up cloth in her hands, wondering why she wasn't drying the bowls.

With his face turned towards her, the setting sun lit one side of his face. His hair wasn't completely black, this close and in this light. There were faint streaks of gold. His scar was obvious. She could see the different texture of the skin where there was no stubble. He had long eyelashes. He was closer than last night.

"The setting sun on your face, your hair." He reached up and stroked her hair over her ear. "You are so beautiful." He bent down.

She waited for the kiss, but he hesitated, waiting for her. His eyes were open, patient. She tilted her head up and touched her lips to his. She closed her eyes, focusing on the warmth where her lips met his. He touched her shoulders, and she leaned in to him, deepening the kiss and parting her lips.

This felt good. Dylan was not an aggressive kisser, trying to get his tongue down her throat. They tasted each other, gently probing with tips of tongues, while his hands settled on her back. She placed her hands on his hips, on the loose sweatpants, and realized she was still holding a cloth. She tossed it away, not seeing where it landed, then stroked her fingers up his back, feeling the ripples of his muscles through the shirt. They deepened the kiss. He rubbed his palms up her back and to her sides, barely brushing the sides of her breasts before slipping back and up to cup her shoulders. He shifted his body away, putting space between them except where their mouths still explored.

She moved towards him and realized why he'd moved back. His erection was obvious through the baggy sweatpants. His only underwear was drying by the stove, and if he was wearing anything under the sweatpants it was loose-fitting. She suppressed a giggle and stepped back, breaking the kiss. She put her hands on the counter to steady herself. They both looked out the window at the sun setting over the ocean.

"Beautiful," Dylan said.

"Yes," said Marianna. "That's one of the reasons I love it here."

They watched the last rays of the sun drop over the horizon. It was quiet, and dark. "I'd better light some candles," said Marianna. Cerebus stood up, stretched, and went to stand beside the door. "You need out?"

He barked.

"Well, it's still raining."

"It may have stopped," said Dylan. "It's quiet."

Marianna opened the door to the porch, and the outer door. Cerebus pushed past her. She followed him onto the deck. The rain had stopped. It was cooler than the fire-warmed kitchen, and she took a deep breath. What had happened in there? She hadn't enjoyed a kiss like that since ... she tried to remember if any of Troy's kisses had stormed her senses.

Dylan came out to the deck. "At last, the storm is gone."

"It was only two days," said Marianna. "Not that long."

"Perhaps not, but it was intense," said Dylan. "Glad that's over."

"It may not be over." Marianna looked up to discern if this was a temporary break, or the weather was clearing. Several stars were visible through the thinning clouds. "Even if it is," said Marianna, "they've still got to fix the road and restore the power. We're not out of the woods yet."

"I'm sure everything will be set by morning," said Dylan.

"You're not from around here, are you," teased Marianna.

"So, I might be stuck here a little longer? Right now, I'm not sure that's such a bad thing." Dylan walked over to her and took her hand. "Now, where were we?" Marianna backed up to the railing, turned, and looked over the ocean.

"Slow down there, mister. That was a nice kiss, and thank you, but it was just a kiss. Let's not get carried away." She was unsure if she was telling him or herself. "It's been a long day. I'm beat. I'm going up to my room. Thanks again for your help today." She backed away. "Good night." She called Cerebus and went inside.

Filling a jug of water in the kitchen, she saw him standing still on the deck, looking out over the ocean. That was not just a kiss, she thought. If that had just been a kiss, she would have invited him up, like she'd done a few times before with attractive single campers, and enjoyed a pleasant evening. This was different, and not just because he wasn't leaving in the morning. He couldn't leave in the morning. She went through the living room, into the office, and picked up bathroom supplies for him. Hopefully, he would not have any reason to knock on her door. She trusted him enough to let him stay in the house, but what was he hiding? He hadn't been hesitant, or aggressive, but confident. That was it, she realized. A little too confident, like he knew her much better than he let on. And now he was trapped here and sleeping in her house. By chance, and by my invitation, she reminded herself. But she'd use the bolt lock on her door tonight, and Cerebus would be with her. He'd proven himself useful against unwanted attention more than once.

12

∽∾

Chapter 12

Dylan woke with the sun warming his face. He opened his eyes, registered that he was in Marianna's spare bedroom and the sun was shining, and closed his eyes again. This was much more comfortable than the previous night in the truck, and the night before in the tent. The cotton flannel sheets were soft and smelled of salt. The house was quiet, and he could hear the waves through the open window. It was the same sound he had fallen asleep to last night.

Last night he'd kissed Marianna. He still was not sure why. No, he knew why. He was attracted to her. But she lived four-teen-hundred kilometres from Toronto, in the middle of nowhere, and now was not a good time to start a relationship. Especially with someone he planned to steal land from. No, it wasn't stealing, he reminded himself. It was business. She knew the terms; she'd signed the document. And this was the deal that would secure his future.

He'd grown up in a house where the mice and rats scampered through gaps in the stone basement walls. His sister probably still lived in a house like that. His first apartment in Toronto had mice running from one radiator to the next. It wasn't the specks of mouse shit on the counters, annoying as it was, or the need to keep all food in rodent-proof containers, that made mice annoying. It was the poverty the mice reminded you of. Of being too poor to fix your house, or too tired from working long hours, or renting and knowing even if you had the money to spend on fixing the place you might have to move next month. Money was security.

He thought of his condo, peaceful and rodent free. He could leave a chocolate bar on the counter, half-eaten, and it would be untouched the next day. This was the happiness money bought. Yvonne had liked the condo, and loved the view of Lake Ontario, visible in a gap between the waterfront towers. He wondered what Marianna would think of that view, compared to her property. He imagined showing his place to her. Would she appreciate the double-size shower and the soaker tub? He closed his eyes and imagined her there. Relaxing in a bubble bath. He'd come in, and she'd put down her book. He'd offer to wash her back. She'd sit up, her breasts emerging from the bubbles, and as he stroked her back with the cloth, he'd lean down and kiss the top of her breasts .... Damn morning wood, he thought, as his erection pressed against the bedding. He threw off the sheets and quilt. His attempt to cool his feelings with chilly air failed in the warmth of the room. Why was his first kiss with Marianna—his only kiss, not his first—more comfortable and yet more exciting than kissing Yvonne, even after all their time together? That thought was enough to distract him.

He put on the baggy sweatpants and tight shirt from yesterday, padded to his door, and opened it. He could hear Marianna in the kitchen, calling Cerebus for breakfast. Marianna's bedroom door was closed. He resisted the temptation to investigate her bedroom and stepped through the landing's open door to the bathroom. She'd filled the jug of water on the counter for handwashing and toothbrushing and added another note to the tips and reminders from last night. This one invited him to shave in the kitchen if he wanted hot water. He brushed his teeth, then picked up a towel and cloth. She'd also left out a couple of disposable razors and a bar of shaving soap.

As he came down the stairs, the temperature increased. In the kitchen, something sweet was cooking on the stove, and cool salt air breezed through an open window. Marianna was setting the table, for two, he noticed, unsure how he felt about that.

"Good morning, Dylan. Did you sleep okay?"

"Yes, thanks. And thanks for all the notes, and the toiletries. Did you sleep well?"

"Apart from letting Cerebus out to pee at two in the morning, yes. He didn't wake you with his barking?"

Dylan shook his head. "You're sure you don't mind me shaving at the kitchen sink?"

"As long as you clean up after yourself." She poured steaming water from a pot on the stove into a bowl and set the bowl beside the sink. "The first cupboard on the left has a mirror inside."

Dylan opened the cupboard. "All mod cons."

"This isn't my first rodeo."

Dylan shaved, deciding he did not want to ask what that

meant. In the mirror, he watched Marianna move about the kitchen, then position herself at the stove.

"Whatever you're making smells good."

"Thanks. Just oatmeal. But I'm heating some maple syrup to go with it. Also boiling some eggs for our hike."

Her hips were swaying as she stirred the pot. Dylan shifted the cupboard door, so the mirror no longer reflected her. "Our hike?"

"I started the generator earlier and was on my radio. The storm was nasty all over the island. Lots of power lines down, and several road washouts. A couple of motels flooded, and the boardwalk is damaged in Sydney. It will be some time before the road out here is repaired. Maybe a week."

"A week? With no power?" Dylan finished his ablutions and came over to the stove. "Are you going to be okay?"

"I'll be fine. I've got the generator, I can run my laptop on solar, I'll have internet once they get the cell tower fixed, which could be before or after the road, I've got the woodstove for heat and cooking, and I've got food. I wouldn't survive winter here if I couldn't go a week on my own. Put that on the table, please, and take a seat." She indicated a small pot. "We just need to get you home."

"Right. I'm stranded here."

Marianna brought the pot of oatmeal to the table and spooned some into the bowl in front of Dylan.

"Don't panic, city boy." He caught her grin. "One of the guys from Bay St. Lawrence can get you out by boat. Say when."

"That's good, thanks." Yvonne had never cooked breakfast for him, but then he'd never stayed for breakfast. Marianna spooned oatmeal into her bowl, took the pot to the sink, and came back to the table. He waited until she had poured some maple syrup, then poured some on his. "This is superb." He'd had maple syrup flavoured instant oatmeal, but this, cooked in a pot and with real maple syrup, tasted so much better it was like a different meal.

"Thanks. But no one can come today. Tomorrow at the earliest. They've got cleanup there too. It'll be a few days before anyone could drive you into Baddeck or Sydney."

"Can't I rent a car, or get the bus, from the village?"

"No. Not anywhere around here. Someone might be able to put you up there, but Mike said you're better to stay here if I've got room."

"Who's Mike?" Dylan reminded himself he had no reason to be jealous.

"Buddy of mine in Bay St. Lawrence. Lobster fisher and does construction in the off-season. He and his sons framed the shelter. He's a got a shortwave radio, so he's my village contact when the phones are out. And he's married, and old enough to be my father. I know that look."

She took a spoonful of oatmeal, swallowed, and continued. "Anyway, you've been here two and a half days, two of which have been heavy rain, and had all your stuff washed away in a flood. I hate to see what the online review will look like. It's a gorgeous day today, and one attraction of this campground is the hike up the mountain behind us. For you, guided, lunch included, just to make it more attractive."

"Your company is more than sufficiently attractive without food and guiding. But the exercise will help take my mind off other things we could do to pass the time." He shouldn't be flirting with her, he thought, but he liked her plan to spend the day together.

Marianna blushed. "Dylan, you are a great kisser. But as I said last night, it was just a kiss. It's not going to lead to anything. I'm not interested in a relationship, and even if I was, you'll be heading back to your downtown Toronto office soon enough. Let's keep things as friends. Okay?" She held out her hand.

Dylan was about to say he'd just been kidding, but he hadn't, and she knew it, and she was right. He shook her hand.

"Agreed, Ms. Berksen."

"How do you know my last name?"

Dylan knew her name from her file but scrambled to come up with another possible explanation. "Susan at the Co-op mentioned it."

"Just call me Marianna, please."

* * *

It's a perfect day, thought Marianna. She lay on a patch of grass, in the shade of a tree, looking over the ocean. Dylan was on the other side of the tree, though still in the shade, and Cerebus was between them, at the edge of the slope.

"Will he go down there?" Dylan asked.

"No. He always stays close." The clearing extended down a gentle slope for about thirty feet, then brush and trees filled an area that fell away to the ocean, hundreds of feet below. Behind them, denser and taller trees obscured the view into a ravine. The last stretch of the trail to the clearing was along a mountain ridge, with breathtaking views on both sides.

"It's an amazing place. 'A fine and private place'," said Dylan.

Marianna responded without thinking. "'But none, I think, do there embrace.'" Marianna wondered if he was flirting again. Finishing the line would hardly discourage him. He'd agreed to just be friends, which was good. Sensible, if disappointing. Now he was quoting love poetry, or perhaps lust poetry.

"Sorry, I didn't mean anything by it. It just came to mind. Bit grim, actually, since he's talking about the grave."

"I know Marvell," said Marianna, "but I'm surprised you do."

"Now who is making assumptions about education?" Dylan sat up. "Just because I got a commerce degree doesn't mean I'm illiterate. I know 'To His Coy Mistress.' Shouldn't be a surprise, since it's the most well-known of the *carpe diem* poems."

Marianna sat up. "You learned that in commerce? We didn't do any poetry in my program."

"We didn't in mine either. I read poetry for fun. It's great reading when you lead a busy life."

"And you appreciate the perspective after a day of slaving over spreadsheets?"

"That, and it's short. Easy to read on the streetcar. And the copyrights have expired on classic poems, so they are free. Legally." Marianna laughed, added this information to the Dylan pro column, and wished there was more on the con side. The distance is a deal-breaker, she reminded herself. "We should be heading back. A different trail, if that's okay with you?"

"Sure."

Marianna double-checked the clearing to ensure they left

nothing behind. Having eaten lunch, their packs were lighter. She moved one water bottle from Dylan's pack to hers, to even the loads. They left the clearing on the trail opposite where they had arrived. Cerebus led the way but was never out of sight. Dylan followed, and Marianna brought up the rear, feeling she should keep an eye on him. It wasn't a chore. Not that the oversized sweatpants or loose kangaroo jacket revealed anything, but she'd seen him topless, and could imagine what he looked like. She imagined him with a sheen of sweat on his chest, though he managed the relaxed pace without apparent effort. He stepped easily on the trail, managing tree roots and areas still muddy from the storm with an ease unexpected for a city dweller. He obviously worked out, but a treadmill is not the same as hiking.

She still sensed that he was hiding something, and she wanted to know what it was. They'd talked little on the way up, absorbing the view and saving breath for the steep trail sections. The return loop was downhill, gentler, and, being in the trees, offered few views. More chance to chat.

"You seem comfortable on rough trails," she said. "Not what I expected from a city boy."

"There's a whole network of parks with trails along the Don Valley Parkway and the ravines leading into it. I often run there. You can forget you are in downtown Toronto, except for the traffic noise and fumes. Didn't you grow up in Toronto?"

"Yes. Actually, North York, but people who didn't live there didn't know it existed, because the mailing addresses always used the name of the former villages, like Willowdale and Downsview."

"I've never heard of North York," said Dylan, "but I have heard of Downsview."

"Now it's all amalgamated into Toronto. Anyway, Mum wasn't from Toronto, and we didn't explore much. I knew my neighbourhood and downtown." Marianna wanted to shift the conversation back to learning about Dylan. "How did you get from poverty on the south shore to being a CPA with an office job in downtown Toronto?" He didn't respond at first, and she was unsure if he had not heard her or was not sure what to say.

"Hard work. And luck." He paused, determined the best route around a muddy area, and started to the left.

"Stop." She pointed to a patch of low bushes. "That's poison ivy. Might not be a problem with the long pants, but let's not risk it. Follow Cere's tracks. It's muddier, but safer."

"Thanks." He followed the path she recommended. "When I was fifteen, I got a cleaning job at a mall. Floors, washrooms, tables in the food court, that sort of thing. It was easy work, but I did it well. I took it more seriously than some other workers. The mall gave me more hours, and I helped a maintenance guy. He taught me how to do simple tasks like replace leaking taps and broken electrical outlets. That gave him more time to drink in the office. One day he groped a saleswoman at the lingerie store and got fired. I got his job full-time, but the mall let me work evenings and weekends, and my teachers didn't mind if I missed a class or two for work. The mall was owned by a big property management company. I kept an eye on the job openings they posted, took some business classes, and just before I graduated, I applied for a job as a mail clerk in the company's Toronto head office. I think they gave it to me because they figured if someone would move from Nova Scotia to Toronto to be a mail clerk, they must really want the job. I shared a crappy apartment, but worked hard, got some promotions, and went to university part-time."

Dylan stopped for a drink of water. Marianna had one too. She wiped her mouth with the back of her hand and noticed that her movement caught his eye. He looked away and started walking again.

"The company got bought out, merged, and downsized. I had no trouble getting another job, but my new company went through the same thing six months later. By then I was working on my CPA. Finally finished it last year, two more companies later. I like the work, and the money's good, but I'm planning to start my own business. That's the only way to job security."

Marianna digested this. "I can appreciate having your own business, but I don't know how secure it is. This place is mortgaged to the hilt. But I'm still growing. Next year I should break even, and after that it should be enough to support me."

Ahead of her, Dylan stumbled over a root. "Are you okay?"

"Yes. Mind that one." He pointed down. "You told me this was your grandmother's place. How did you get from an office job in downtown Toronto to here?

She wondered how much to tell him. But she had no reason to keep secrets, and he'd told her everything about himself. "I told you my dad left." Or died? She needed to talk to her mother. "Mum worked while I was in school. I was a latchkey kid. Let myself in after school because Mum was at work. There was a stay-at-home mum next door, and she kept an eye on me. Same if Mum had to go out at night. But during the summers Mum didn't want me home all day, so she sent me out to stay with Grandma. Paying for the trip was cheaper than paying a sitter. Take the path to the left. Cere! This way!"

Dylan paused, to let Cerebus resume the lead.

"Sounds like fun."

"I didn't like it the first year. All my friends were playing soccer, and I had to stay with someone I didn't know, on a farm in the middle of nowhere. But by the end of the summer, I didn't want to leave. I came out every year from when I was five to when I was fifteen. That year I wanted to stay with my friends, and it didn't matter that Mum was working."

"How was your grandmother with that?"

"She never complained, but I know she missed me. And by the end of that summer, I realized I missed her, and the ocean. That year I came out over Thanksgiving. Saw the colours for the first time. After that, I started coming out at different times of the year, usually for a week."

"Living out here, she must have loved the company."

"She liked living on her own. When she got older, I suggested she sell the place and move into Bay St. Lawrence, or maybe to a home in Sydney, but she wouldn't hear of that. She hired a man sometimes to help with things around the house." From the way Grandma spoke of her helper, Marianna suspected the hired man had been a more intimate companion than Grandma was willing to admit.

"Was her name Kate?"

"Yes. How did you know?"

Dylan stopped and held a tree branch out of the way. "There's a book in your living room, with a somewhat salacious title, that was a gift to her from someone with the initials E. G. D. The hired man, perhaps?"

"Thanks." Marianna caught the branch and slipped it behind her. "Maybe. She never told me his name, but whenever he came up in conversation, which was rare, she'd stress that she was too old to be dating, which made me suspicious. She also told me he wasn't from anywhere nearby, because then there would be gossip. I'm sure there was anyway, with her on her own much of the time. I'm sure there is about me too, though since I employ a few folks here, no one would dare say anything to my face."

"You told me about coming out to visit, but how did you end up moving out here?"

"She asked me once, a few years before she died, if I wanted the house. I told her I was happy in Toronto, and we'd sell it when she died, since Mum needed the money." Marianna remembered that discussion. It had been the only time she and her grandmother had argued. Marianna had accused her grandmother of being cruel to her daughter, and her grandmother had insisted Marianna's mother had no need of money, and that the property should stay in the family. Maybe there was more to the disagreement between her mother and grandmother.

"But you didn't sell it."

"Grandma left enough money to my mum that there was no urgent need to sell the house. Mum was able to pay all her debts. She bought some new furniture, and a newer car, and invested the rest for her retirement. Non-cashable investment certificates, of various terms," she added, in response to Dylan's questioning look. "Not very exciting, but safe. We don't know for sure how she accumulated the money, but I learned her property used to be larger. I always thought it was the cleared area plus a few hundred metres in each direction, but it used to continue along the waterfront, including this area."

"Who owns this now?" asked Dylan.

"It's Crown land. After Grandma sold it, there were several numbered companies that bought and sold it. One defaulted on taxes, and the government seized it when the owners couldn't be found."

"Would you want to buy it back?"

"I'm happy with it being Crown land. It's remote enough that hunters are rare and city folks with toys, dirt bikes, ATVs, and snow machines don't bother coming here." Me owning it wouldn't stop them anyway, Marianna thought. "But if it comes up for sale, I'd like to buy it, if I could afford it. Ideally, it would become a protected wilderness area. I've written the minister to request that."

"That wouldn't cost you anything and would enhance the value of your campground. Good move. What about the campground and the house?"

"Grandma left that to me. The house was in good shape, but the land was mostly overgrown pasture. My first impulse was to list it for sale when I came out for the funeral, but that seemed too soon. I hired a couple in from Bay St. Lawrence to maintain it and keep watch on the place. I didn't want anyone to think it was an abandoned property. I came out a few months later to arrange for the sale, but decided I wanted one more summer visit here. Then I planned to sell it so that my fiancé and I could get a condo in Toronto. You know what happened there. Then I was laid off. I couldn't afford my apartment and I didn't want to move back in with Mum. Besides, she'd taken a smaller apartment when I moved out. I came out here to think about what to do next and stayed."

"You had some rough times. Great accomplishment on your part to take over the property and make it into a source of income."

Marianna realized her tale of woe included inheriting property, while Dylan had started with less and not had that benefit, but he didn't point that out. "Eventually," she said.

"I'm glad we didn't come up this way. Even going down is a challenge in spots. Did you put up the ropes?"

"Yes. We're almost at the bottom. There's a short, steep climb, then it clears, and we'll be out of the shade." Marianna didn't tell him what was up ahead.

13

Chapter 13

Exercise is supposed to take your mind off women, thought Dylan, but it doesn't work when you are exercising with a woman. Especially one as attractive and smart as Marianna. There had been a moment, after lunch, under the tree, when he wanted nothing more than to crawl across the ground to her and kiss her. It was a "fine and private place," in the woods, looking over the ocean, though Dylan was not sure how Cerebus would react to the activity. And she was right. He was going back to Toronto. But maybe he should seize the day. "Had we but time enough." They were both adults, both single. Why not enjoy a few hours of each other's company? His two experiences with one-night stands had been years ago, with women he had just met, and probably wouldn't like if he did get to know them. With Yvonne, they had dated for months, though infrequently, before going to bed. Dating Marianna wasn't feasible, however much he might want to, nor was it reasonable at this point in his career. But he knew her and liked her. A one-night stand might be fine. And perhaps more than one night, depending how long he was stranded here.

While he was mulling over the possibility, she had stood up and suggested they carry on. It's for the best, thought Dylan. He banished the thought of making a pass at her and got up to follow. Only the thought did not stay banished as they hiked through the woods.

Without looking back, he was aware of her a few feet behind him. He could hear her breathing on the more challenging sections of the path, her soft footfalls, and sometimes a musky fragrance. She wore little makeup, as far as he could tell. Would she have put on fragrance for a hike? More likely a deodorant. He didn't have his, of course, and he hadn't showered since getting caught in the rain yesterday. He'd managed a quick wipe at the sink earlier, and the easy hike in shade meant he wasn't sweating much. The shaving cream she had provided for him was not his preferred scent, but it was better than nothing.

Talking about family and property was a safe topic, and he learned Marianna did not have surplus land to sell. That her mother moved to a smaller apartment confirmed there was no family money available. This was promising for the deal, though he did not feel as pleased as he should have. When she talked about her family, she mentioned her father had left. Had she read the letter? He did not want to ask her.

After the promised brief but steep climb, the trees thinned and opened to a large clearing. Dylan almost stumbled on the level ground and paused. The clearing overlooked a sheltered narrow bay. A pit in the clearing distracted from the natural beauty. He caught up with Marianna, walking towards the pit, and they stopped at the edge of it. It was a large rectangle, about thirty feet along the side where he was standing, stretching into the distance several hundred feet. He looked closer. Under the brush of the clearing edge, he recognized the concrete walls of a foundation. The mounds in the bottom of the pit were not just dirt and weeds, but pieces of burned wood and rusted steel beams.

"What is this place? What happened here?" It looked like a resort that had burned down, but the road had ended at Marianna's campground. There was no sign of a road here. And this was Marianna's grandmother's property before she sold it.

"Remember I said that numbered companies bought the property before it became Crown land?"

Dylan nodded.

"One of them started this resort, about ten or fifteen years ago. It was supposed to be a playground for the wealthy, reachable only by boat. The government put up a bunch of cash, and construction started, but the place was never finished. Eventually it burned down. Arson, of course. By then everyone knew the whole project was a complex land fraud, with money laundering and tax evasion tossed in. A few locals who worked on it never got paid, and no one knows if one of them burned it down or if the owners did, for the insurance. There were lawsuits, but apparently no one could ever be found to be charged. Ownership always ended up getting traced to another company or another country, and the trail went cold. Eventually everyone gave up and cut their losses, and the government seized the land. The government gave a Halifax company a few million to clean the place and haul away the debris, but they went out of business without doing anything. Such a waste." She started walking again.

Dylan followed her. He could see why they had picked this spot for the resort. Nestled between steep green hills, with trees down to a sheltered cove, and the open ocean beyond, the view was magnificent. She was right. This was a waste.

"That was the pool there." They skirted another, smaller opening, filled with debris and leaves, and down a set of concrete stairs to a partially completed concrete boardwalk. The beach was rocky, with loose shale.

"Not much of a beach," said Dylan. "Not sandy like yours."

"No. That's probably why no one else wanted to buy the land. From what I read, there was never any intention to complete the resort. It's scenic, but isolated. No road, and the bay is hazardous. At low tide you can see shale rocks all over the harbour."

A set of concrete piers stretched out into the sheltered cove. "This was part of the dock. The trail is along the beach for a bit, then back into the woods."

The beach ended at a rocky cliff. Cerebus turned into the woods, as if he were reading the pink arrow spray-painted on the rocks. Dylan stopped. He looked back at the beach, the partly constructed boardwalk, and the clearing. From here, there was no sign of the foundations or piles of charred debris. But the land was scarred. Marianna walked up to him, then turned to share his view.

"What a mess, eh? How does something like that happen?" She faced him. "Ready to climb more? We've got to go up a bit to get out of this ravine, but it's mostly flat after that. We're halfway back." Cerebus trotted back to them and barked.

"Thanks for showing me this. Okay, Cerebus, lead on."

Dylan had never considered himself an environmentalist.

The projects his company built were mostly on previously built properties, and, in a city, what difference did it make if a nine- or fifteen-storey building replaced a four-storey building? He'd heard how easy it was to sway anti-development councillors. But here, in the remote woods of Cape Breton Island, a large development did not fit. And this wasn't even a real development. It was just a scam, or a series of scams. Much like what would happen to Marianna's property once he called in her loan. The possible fate of Marianna's property, burned-out ruins and a scar in the landscape, preoccupied Dylan for the rest of the hike, though he appreciated a stop for wild raspberries.

The power was still out at the house. Marianna insisted on preparing dinner without help. Dylan retreated to the living room, respecting her need for alone time. He checked the floor under the table. She had picked up the letter. He looked over the shelves but could not see it. She may have put it away without reading it, but last night she had been distracted when she'd come back into the kitchen. She'd barely said anything until they had started talking about old TV shows. He couldn't ask if she had read the letter without revealing that he had read it. She might talk about it when she was ready. Not that it was his problem, he reminded himself. He picked up *The Blue Lagoon* but could not pay attention to the story. It wasn't Cerebus snoring on the floor in front of the fireplace. Dylan was trying to work out a way to save his deal and Marianna's property. I'm not trying to impress her, he told himself, it's just the right thing to do. I don't even believe that myself, he thought. But none of the scenarios he imagined worked out for both of them, so he could not impress her even if he wanted to.

14

⌒

Chapter 14

It was dark when Cerebus woke Marianna with a single bark. He waited at her bedroom door, needing out. She considered donning a robe to let him out but decided Dylan might be up and she should be properly dressed. Yes, I should be, she reminded herself, her mind briefly wandering. It was warmer than yesterday, so she skipped a bra in favour of a heavy cotton tank top. Almost properly dressed, she thought, but I should be comfortable in my own house.

Cerebus rushed past her at the doors, relieved himself on the post railing at the bottom of the stairs, and then began an examination of the area around the house. The pink glow on the eastern horizon showed dawn was near. Might as well stay up, thought Marianna, and closed the door. Cerebus could explore for a while. She built up the fire in the stove and considered baking bread, and muffins for breakfast.

Dylan had been preoccupied with something last night. She tried to imagine what it was. He was quiet through dinner. She could not remember what they had discussed, but whatever it was, they had said little. Perhaps he was tired from the hike, or uncomfortable with being trapped at the campground—or trapped in the cozy domestic setting of being a couple sharing dinner and dishes again. It was seductive. She recognized the desire for a relationship, as she had during the years of her secret relationship with Troy, but with Dylan there was a comfortable quiet connection that had not existed with Troy.

While Dylan had done the dishes, she'd run the generator long enough to cool down the fridge, and then the freezer, and checked with Mike on the radio. His boat was out of commission, but he'd said Gerry would come out the day after tomorrow. When she passed that news on to Dylan, he'd seemed resigned, likely resenting the delay. They played two games of Scrabble, and she won both, though the second was close. That did not improve his mood, but she wouldn't let him win to soothe his male ego. And he said he enjoyed playing. There was something in his eyes when they said good night on the landing, something he did not want to tell her, but she didn't press him, or give in to the temptation to give him a hug. He could misinterpret that, and she'd agreed to be friends only. Just before she went to sleep, she had remembered her concern that he was hiding something.

As she mixed dough, she considered what he had told her, and whether she still thought he was hiding something. Half an hour later, when she took the muffins out of the oven, she still wasn't sure. On her second muffin, she wondered if Troy had made her too suspicious of men.

She heard the toilet flush upstairs, and Dylan came down a few moments later. He was wearing a pair of shorts that were snug enough to see the outlines of his underwear, and a loose-fitting, faded Blue Nose Marathon Volunteer T-shirt.

"Smells delicious down here. Is that something for breakfast?"

"Blueberry muffins. I already had one or two. Help yourself." She waved at the plate on the counter.

"This is great. Thanks. I must say I'm eating much better than if I'd been getting my own meals."

"You're practically my hostage here. Least I can do."

He came to stand beside her at the sink. Her pulse quickened, remembering the kiss when they stood here before.

"I should be doing the dishes, though." He didn't try to take over but didn't move away either. She considered tossing him the cloth and decided to stand her ground.

"I'm not used to having someone around." That did not sound as firm as she had intended.

"Of course." He nodded and moved away, turning to look out a window.

She should have thrown the cloth at him, she thought, for not taking her response as an invitation to flirt, not that she had intended that. Then she reminded herself that she had turned him down, and he was respecting that. Damn if that didn't make him more appealing. She watched him lick a stray chunk of blueberry from his upper lip, then take another bite. No harm in watching, she thought. A piece of muffin broke as he was biting, and he tried to capture it with his tongue. *Oh my.* The crumb escaped and fell to the floor. "Don't worry, Cerebus can get that." She looked around.

"Where is he?" Dylan said. "Shouldn't he be here, begging for a morsel?"

"He's still outside." Marianna ran to the porch door, and into the porch. "I can't believe he didn't bark." She opened the outer door. "Cere? Cere! Where are you?" She stepped onto the stairs, and Dylan followed. "Cere!" She ran back into the porch, slipped on rubber boots, and ran down to the yard. "Cere!" She walked all around the house, calling his name. When she came back to the door, Dylan was still at the porch. "Cere's gone!"

Dylan did not appreciate her concern. "He'll be here in a moment."

"You don't understand. I put him out over an hour ago, but now he's gone. I can't see him anywhere. He knows not to leave the campground area without me, and even if he chased a rabbit into the woods, he wouldn't go far, and he'd run back the moment I called."

"Let's go look for him." Dylan put his runners on and came down the porch stairs. "Walk the perimeter of the campground?"

"Sure. Let's start down at the beach."

Marianna dashed for the staircase down to the beach and heard Dylan close behind her. There was no sign of Cerebus anywhere, but she called him several times. She walked down to the wet sand near the water, looking for footprints. There were none. She started walking east along the beach. Dylan stayed at the bottom of the stairs, looking out at the surf for a few minutes, then ran to catch up with her.

"He wouldn't go out in the water?"

"No," said Marianna. "He hates the water."

"I'll sure he'll be fine. We'll find him soon."

"You don't even like dogs."

"Well, no. But that doesn't mean I wish him harm." Dylan lowered his voice. "And I don't like to see you unhappy."

Marianna was not sure what to make of that remark, but now was not the time to be distracted by whatever there was or was not between them. It was her mooning over Dylan that had led her to forget Cerebus outside. She walked away from the water, closer to the embankment at the top of the beach, and called for Cerebus again.

When they arrived back at the house an hour later, after making a detour to confirm Cerebus was not at the washroom building, Marianna was near tears. They stood at the foot of the stairs to the porch.

"Come in for a few minutes." Dylan took her arm. "I'll make you some tea. Then we can go out again."

"I don't want tea. I want Cere!" Marianna shook his arm free and took a step back. "And don't 'poor woman' me. Damn it. Cerebus!"

* * *

Dylan tried offering more search suggestions, but Marianna got more upset. Frustrated at his inability to reassure her with words, he stepped forward and hugged her. "It will be okay." She was stiff in his arms, then sobbed a moment, relaxed, and wrapped her arms around him. He had the notion that everything would be okay. The dog would be found, her campground would be saved, he'd have his job. Standing with her, the most pressing sensation was not her hands on his back, or her head and breasts he felt against his chest, but that it would all work out, somehow. He hoped her relaxing into the embrace meant she felt the same. He stepped back. "You okay?"

She sniffed and did not meet his eyes. "Yes, thanks."

"Come in for a break. Just a few minutes. Warm up. I'll make that tea. Then we'll find him."

They decided she should stay at the house, just in case Cerebus came back. She'd scan the campground with binoculars while he walked the perimeter, checking deeper into the surrounding woods. Dylan, this time wearing the oversized sweatpants, kangaroo jacket, and rubber boots, explored every possible path from the campground, and used a stick to push aside low branches and brush.

As he searched, he considered the problem of the campground. For years, he had solved this kind of problem using a spreadsheet. Punch in some numbers, build an equation, and see the results. Then he'd try different numbers, or a different equation, until the best scenario was obvious. With no power, and not even his phone, it was hard to focus on the numbers. What he wanted, or didn't want, was clouding the view.

The only way to save the Sandcastle Rock Campground and protect Marianna was for her to pay off the loan. She didn't have the money. She couldn't borrow it. Her credit rating was poor, and she did not have any family to borrow from except her mother, who apparently had money but couldn't access it easily. Since her mother hadn't loaned her money in the first place, there might not be that much, or her mother might not be willing to give it to Marianna. He wondered if she could crowd fund. Probably not the amount required. The only connection she had with money was him.

He could loan her the money. He didn't have the cash unless he sold his condo. It would wipe him out, without enough to set up an office. And if he helped a debtor pay a debt, not only would he not get a bonus, he'd also be fired. Her campground could be the first investment of his new company. But it was a shaky foundation, and if word got out that he'd poached a client to start his own firm, other investors might be hard to sign up. He'd have no office and nowhere to live, at least until he found an apartment. That was not an easy task in Toronto, and it would be harder if he was self-employed. He could sell the condo to an investor and rent it back, and work from home, but without an impressive office he would not get the large investors he wanted.

Dylan checked in and around the well house, but there was no sign of Cerebus. He headed back to the edge of the cleared area. "Cerebus!" Nothing. When they'd come this way earlier, they'd explored the faint path under the next tree as far as a steep-edged ravine. Dylan followed the path again, more out of a desire to be methodical than expecting to find anything this time. He walked along the ravine, further from the cleared area. "Cerebus!" He heard a faint whine, coming from the ravine, or was it the breeze? He sat down on the edge and called again. The whine came from below his feet.

Scrambling down, holding onto tree roots, Dylan reached the marshy stream bed. "Cerebus! Found you!" The dog was lying under ferns, hidden from above, and his muddy fur blended with the ground he lay on. Dylan guessed he'd been trying to pull himself up the ravine. He whimpered and wagged his tail when he saw Dylan but did not attempt to get up. There were no obvious injuries. Dylan ran his hands over the dog's body and legs, more to reassure the animal than to diagnose anything. Cerebus squealed in pain when Dylan touched a joint on the left hind leg. Compared to the right leg, the joint was swollen. Dylan wasn't sure if the joint was a dog's knee or ankle or something else, but he knew the dog could not walk.

"Okay, puppy. I'm not going to like this, and you're not going to like this, but I need to carry you back to the house. And the first part will be the hardest. We need to get you out of this ditch."

Dylan petted Cerebus, which relaxed both of them. Then he put his arms around the dog's narrow chest and pulled up. He brought Cerebus to a standing position, held him there with one hand and wrapped the other around the back of the dog's hind legs. He made sure his knees were bent and his back straight, then lifted the dog and held him against his chest.

"No offense puppy, but you are heavier than you look. And you stink." Cerebus whined. Dylan shifted his arms to reduce pressure on the dog's sore leg, and Cerebus yelped. Dylan put the dog down, trying to minimize moving the sore leg. He took off his kangaroo jacket and tucked it under the dog, using the jacket as a sling in front of the dog's hind legs, then picked up Cerebus again. The dog's hind legs hung freely while Dylan held the sling with one hand high and kept his other hand low under the dog's chest.

"That better?" Dylan took a few steps. Cerebus did not whine or squirm. "Okay. I can't climb up carrying you, so we're going to have to walk along this streambed until the bank is lower. Which way?"

Dylan looked both ways, and wished he knew something about finding your way in the woods. He should have brought a whistle, or a compass, or both. It looked like the embankment was parallel to the upper boundary of the cleared camping area, so it didn't matter which way he went, as long as he didn't go too far. The ravine sloped, and down would be easier, but it might cut deeper as it went. He started walking uphill in the ravine, placing each foot in turn on the slippery ground.

"You got any ideas about how I can avoid taking this away from Marianna?" Cerebus looked up at him. "Of course not. You're just a silly dog." Cerebus licked Dylan's hand. "I'm so mixed up about that woman I'm talking to a dog. Delirium must be setting in."

The morning had been cool, but even in the shade of the woods it was getting warmer. Dylan's chest, where Cerebus pressed against it, was wet.

Dylan started to worry he'd go past the edge of the campground when, on the other side of a boulder twice his height, the ravine became undistinguishable from the uneven ground and the view opened. Through the trees, he could see the ocean in the distance, and turned in that direction. He could not walk in a straight line, due to fallen trees and pits in the ground, but, orienting himself to the ocean, he walked towards what he hoped was the campground.

"Break time, puppy." He stopped, and placed Cerebus on the ground, putting the sore leg down gently. "Don't run away now." The dog lay on the ground, panting. "Yes, I know. I should have brought water. I could use some myself. 'This is some rescue.' That's from *Star Wars*. Still remember when my dad showed me that movie. Insisted we watch a fuzzy videotape instead of a DVD, for some reason. Said it was more authentic. I don't know why you are panting when I'm doing all the work." Dylan stretched, and flexed his arms. He could hear surf, so they must be close to the water, but he should have been at the camping area by now. "Let's go, before she has to send out a search party for me. As if she could contact anyone. Is she foolish or courageous for living out here?" He picked up Cerebus and continued heading towards the ocean.

15

∾

Chapter 15

Marianna checked her watch. She hadn't seen Dylan for over an hour. He'd disappeared into the bush at the hill and not come out. Was he lost? Following a trail to Cerebus? Being a city boy, most likely lost. And he'd gone out without any hiking gear. He had no water, no whistle, no compass. He should not be going into the woods without that. She considered trying to follow him, but Cerebus might come back, and he could be hurt. Dylan was an adult. Even if he got lost, he wouldn't panic. As long as he headed for the ocean, he'd be fine. She raised the binoculars and scanned the perimeter of the campground again. No sign of Cerebus or Dylan. She looked higher, in the bush above the campground, but could not see any movement. Should she radio for Search and Rescue? The longer she waited, the more lost Dylan could get. She could at least head up to the perimeter. With the binoculars she could still check the house and come back down if Cerebus came back.

She walked up to the washroom building and checked inside again. No sign of Cerebus. Standing in the shade of the unfinished picnic shelter, she looked down at the house. No sign of Cerebus, but she used the binoculars to be sure. As she put them down, movement to the side caught her eye. Someone was climbing the stairs from the beach. She looked through the binoculars. Dylan—and he was carrying Cerebus.

Marianna ran down to the beach, yelling "Is he okay?" Cerebus looked limp, but Dylan nodded. She could see Cerebus panting as she got closer. Dylan stopped to wait for her and leaned on the post at the top of the stairs.

"His leg is hurt."

"Is he bleeding? Let me see." She petted Cerebus. "You had me so worried."

"Let's get him to the house. I don't think he can walk, but there's no bleeding, and I don't think anything is broken. Sprained, maybe. I don't know if dogs can get sprained."

"Yes, they can." She felt the swelling along the dog's leg. "He must have fallen. Can you bring him up to the house? Thank you, thank you for finding him. Where was he?"

They walked to the house. Dylan carried Cerebus, and Marianna kept one hand on the dog. "Easy boy. Almost home."

"He was at the bottom of a small ravine. He'd been trying to get out. That's why he's so muddy. We checked the ravine earlier, but didn't see him under the brush, or maybe he moved."

"Poor guy. What were you doing, Cerebus?"

"I couldn't carry him and climb out of the ravine, so I had to walk out of it, but I got lost. I ended up past the campground. Came down to the water, and then along the beach. Sorry to take so long."

"I was getting worried about you as well." Marianna opened the doors for Dylan. Dylan carried Cerebus over to his bed in the corner of the kitchen and settled him down. Marianna brought the water bowl closer, so he could drink without getting up. "There you go. Dylan, you must be thirsty too. Don't use water from the pump. Get some from the jug on the counter."

"Should I get some ice?" asked Dylan.

"No. The injury was a few hours ago, and ice is not good for an older dog. There's a pot of warm water on the stove. Could you dip a cloth in that for me? The wood stove," she added, as Dylan looked confused. He got a cloth, dipped it in the pot, and wrung it. He brought it to Marianna, and she weaved it around the sprain.

"Does he need a vet?"

"Probably not. I just need to make sure he rests as much as possible for a few days. Thanks so much." She stood up and moved to hug Dylan. He stepped back.

"Are you sure you want to do that? I must need a shower."

She registered his appearance for the first time. Splattered mud covered him from head to foot. Leaves, twigs, and thistles stuck to his sweatpants, which were torn in places. Sweat soaked his shirt where it wasn't muddy. He even had mud on his forehead, and his hair was plastered with sweat and more mud. She leaned in, touching the sides of his arms with her palms, and brushed his lips. "Thank you."

"You're welcome."

"Can't do a shower. Could do a bath, but it's a warm, for a fall day. You could go for a swim. That would get most of it off."

"That works for me."

"You go ahead. I'll bring down some towels and food."

Marianna packed a bag with sausage, cheese, bread, and pickles. She filled a second bag with beach towels and grabbed a tube of sunscreen. "You stay in your bed and rest." She petted Cerebus and dropped a few treats within reach. "I'll be on the beach for a bit. Back soon." She closed the kitchen door to ensure Cerebus didn't attempt the stairs. On her way out, she picked up a beach umbrella from the porch.

Dylan was waist-deep in the water when she arrived on the beach. He waved, she waved back, and he started swimming. A front crawl, in good form, she thought. Probably swims as part of his workout. The ocean was more challenging than a pool, thanks to waves and current, but the surf was low, and he knifed through it. She tore herself away from the pleasant view.

She set up the umbrella beside his pile of discarded clothes and set out towels on the warm sand. When she sat down, she could see his one pair of underwear tucked into the filthy sweatpants. Was he swimming nude? She glanced out to the ocean. He was swimming back and forth. She couldn't see if he was wearing trunks.

Watching him swim, she remembered her grandmother telling her stories of selkies—seals that took human form. Male selkies were, in her grandmother's words, fine-figured men. Marianna later learned they were also considered powerful seducers of women, seeking out women unhappy with their lives. You could capture a selkie by stealing and hiding their human skin. She looked at the pile of clothes and back to the ocean. "I've already captured all your gear, or the land did. Will that make you stay?" The notion was absurd. He might be from the south shore, but he was a city boy now. He'd never stay. But what would it be like to have someone so entranced they'd give up everything to be with you? Romantic and frightening. One day they'd resent what they had given up.

He was standing again, walking towards the shore. As the water drained back, gathering under and lifting the next wave, she saw he was wearing the snug shorts he'd had on earlier. She was both relieved and disappointed, but even with the silly shorts he looked delicious.

"Thanks." He sat down on a towel. "Not going in yourself?"

"No. I brought some lunch." She opened the bag and took out a pair of metal camping plates. When she brought her lunch to the beach, she always ate from the container, but plates were more appropriate for company.

"You don't like to swim? Living by the ocean?"

"I used to like it when I was a kid. Not so often now. For one thing, it's not safe to go out alone. I thought you'd know better and wait for me."

"Sorry."

"Apology accepted. When campers are here, I'm on the job, so not much swimming then, either."

"You're not alone now, and I'm a friend, remember. Come on out. Join me?" He stood up and held out his hand to help Marianna up.

"I don't have time for this. I should work on the shelter."

"Swim with me now, and I'll help you with the shelter later. And, I don't mean to be rude, but when did you last shower?" He grinned.

"I sponge bathed last night, not that it's any of your business. But okay. I need to cover the food." She covered the plates with a tea towel, weighed it down with water bottles, and accepted his still-offered hand.

"Here we go!" He lifted her and pulled her towards the ocean.

She laughed and followed, protesting. "Hey! Let me change first. I don't want to get these clothes wet!" She was also suddenly conscious of being braless.

"Okay." He stopped, and let her go, then spun behind her and scooped her into his arms, holding her under her knees and back. He held her high, her hip pressed against his firm flat stomach. "You can wash your clothes while you swim." He grinned.

"You really should put me down." She'd never had a brother or close male friend. This casual contact, play, not foreplay, was fun. She put one arm around his neck, warm and wet, and wondered if he would drop her in the ocean. He carried her until he was knee-deep in the water, threatening to drop her the whole time, but not loosening his hold. When he brushed her breast, she assumed it was accidental. She felt safe in his arms. She trusted him not to drop her, and she played along, shrieking with an exaggerated fear of water until she thought he might drop her from laughing. It was foreplay, she realized, but with the emphasis on play, not what may or may not come next. He turned and carried her over to the stairs. He set her down on the landing. "Go get changed. I'll be waiting."

16

∿

Chapter 16

Dylan waited under the beach umbrella while she changed in her house. He was hungry, but his mother's advice to stay out of the water for an hour after eating encouraged him to stay out of the food until after they swam together. He wanted to see Marianna playing in the water. She works too hard, he thought, then reminded himself that he did too. One good thing about the washed-out road was being forced to relax for a few days.

He wondered if she would wear a one-piece or a two-piece. She was practical, and leaned towards comfortable baggy clothing, so a one-piece was more likely. I was right, he thought, when she appeared at the top of the stairs in a blue wave-patterned one-piece. But it was snug, revealing, and her body was everything he'd imagined it was, based on the fuzzy reflection he saw a few days ago, and what he'd felt hugging and holding her. Gorgeous.

She walked past him. "Let's go."

He jumped up and walked beside her. "How's Cerebus?"

"He's fine. Sleeping." As the water reached her knees, she said "It's cold, but not that bad."

"You'll soon get used to it," said Dylan.

"Look at you. One swim in the ocean after years in pools, and the city boy's an expert."

"I was swimming in the Atlantic before you were born."

"No," said Marianna, "but thanks for the compliment."

"You know my age?"

She nodded.

"Yes, of course. The driver's licence when I registered. You have me at a disadvantage." Which was not entirely true, Dylan reminded himself.

"Good." Already in up to her chest, she started swimming. Dylan floated onto his back and paddled his legs. He enjoyed the sun on his chest as he bobbed in the waves, trying to forget the reason he was there.

Lunch was simple and hearty. The morning hike to retrieve Cerebus, and the swims, had left Dylan hungry. The fresh air, beach setting, and gorgeous woman next to him enhanced the meal. He thanked her for the food. She was quiet while they ate, staring out at the waves.

"Looking for the rescue boat to get me out of here?" Dylan asked.

"No. It's coming tomorrow. Didn't I tell you?"

"Yes." But he was looking forward to leaving less and less. And he still had not worked out the solution to her financial challenge. Dylan had sorted out many complex deals. Now he couldn't resolve avoiding a simple demand loan default. No, that wasn't the problem. The problem was he knew the solution, but it made no sense. He'd only known her a few days.

Maybe he'd come up with something this afternoon. "Thanks for the delicious lunch."

"You're welcome. We should work on the shelter now, but that swim tired me more than I thought it would. Swimming obviously uses some muscles that hammering does not." She stretched out her arms and rotated them back and forth to stretch her muscles.

Dylan admired the display and considered offering a massage. He decided she might think that too intimate, or mistake that for an invitation. Or he might mistake her acceptance for an invitation.

"Maybe a short nap," he suggested.

"Good idea." She stretched out on the blanket, in the shade of the umbrella, and closed her eyes. "Wake me in an hour."

He lay on the other side of the umbrella pole, on his side, and watched the rise and fall of her chest. This is a view I could get used to, he thought. He turned onto his other side, facing up the beach. He wished he'd brought a book, though he realized that was avoiding what he needed to think about. How to save the campground, and his job. *Why do I care about it so much? Because I care what happens to her. Why do I care what happens to her? There's nothing between us.* He fell asleep.

The brief nap turned into a lengthy one, and when they awoke it was too late to work on the shelter. Dylan apologized, and Marianna told him no apology was necessary. "When our bodies say we need to sleep, we should listen to them."

They gathered up the picnic items, umbrella, and his clothes, and carried everything back to the house. At the foot of the porch, they used towels to rub off as much sand as possible.

"I'd suggest stripping out here, to avoid bringing sand in, but ...."

She agreed. "Let's respect the friendship boundary, bring a little sand in, and change in our rooms."

The day was still warm. When they both returned to the kitchen, she suggested a picnic dinner on the deck, as the wood-burning stove left the kitchen uncomfortably toasty. She accepted his help for a change, hunger winning out over a desire for alone time, so he washed and cut up carrots while she cut up cheese, bread, and a tinned ham.

"Did you have enough of the pickles at lunch?"

"I can eat more. They're good."

She looked at the assembled food on the platter. "Sorry it's just more of what we ate at lunch. I should get more ambitious with my garden."

"Given that this is the third day without power, and an unexpected guest, I'm impressed with this spread, especially the fresh bread. How long can you go with just the generator?"

"I did a week without power last winter, though I hardly used the generator. Wood for heat and cooking, solar for my phone, and you don't need the fridge when it's freezing outside."

Dylan was again impressed with how resourceful this woman was. She was chattier than usual though, as if she were nervous about something.

"Would you like some wine?" she offered. "That would make it more like dinner. I've got a dry white, a couple of reds, a sparkling rosé—it's a little sweet, but might work with the ham."

"I'll have whatever you choose, thanks." He carried the platter out to the deck, along with napkins. Cerebus followed, favouring his sore leg. Marianna brought out the bottle of wine, and glasses.

* * *

After dinner, they watched the sun set over the ocean. An enjoyable evening, thought Dylan. If it had been a date, it could not have been more perfect. The picnic dinner was casual and familiar, like they'd been together for years instead of days, though they shared childhood memories, as if on a third date. Marianna talked about her childhood summer visits to her grandmother's property, and about how she wanted other children to experience the ocean. "There are beaches in Toronto, on the lake, but it's not the same." Dylan agreed. Compared to the ocean, lake beaches were dull, and did not smell right. He hadn't noticed until this trip.

Dylan told her about his first job. "We lived on a main road, on the way to a beach. No facilities at the beach, like most beaches in this province, so I sold ice cream treats. Started out with a cooler at the foot of the driveway, and by August I'd made enough money to buy a used chest freezer. Hauled it to the end of the driveway, put a lock on it, chained it to a tree, and ran an extension cord from the house. Did that for three summers."

"A budding entrepreneur."

"When I was fifteen, I was old enough to get a real job, so I rented my ice cream business to a couple of buddies. At the end of the season, they bought the freezer for more than I'd paid for it."

"And that's when you started working at the mall?"

"Yes. It was good to get an actual paycheque, but not being able to set my own hours or make my own plans for the work was rough. Almost got fired at the end of my first week, but I settled down and learned to do exactly what I was told. Then I discovered it was easy to exceed expectations. The same co-workers who had encouraged me to do what I was told, also told me not to work too hard, as it made them look bad, but I got promotions, and they didn't. Once I am running my own business again, I'll be working on my own terms again, and this time with a decent income."

Dylan realized he had never told Yvonne about these early struggles, and wondered if that was because she hadn't asked, or because he'd had the notion she didn't care. Yvonne had told him once that his rural life before coming to Toronto was a chapter best forgotten, but sitting on Marianna's deck, watching the sun set over the ocean, and hearing the waves on the beach as the tide came in, he smiled at the memories of those summers.

He'd worked, but not all the time. He'd had free time for long nights at the beach. And those first jobs had been more satisfying than anything he'd done lately. Though those early jobs paid little, setting up the frozen treat stand, then fixing vent fans and balky plumbing, had given him the satisfaction of working with his hands, and seeing the results. That was missing from deskwork, though solving financial problems did pay a lot more. He reminded himself that this campground was a financial problem that needed to be solved. Maybe the deal could be restructured to ensure Marianna got some money out of it. The last stage of the flip was probably worth millions, and his company could set aside more for her and still make a healthy profit.

She interrupted his musing. "I understand the urge to be self-employed, but there's a lot to be said for a regular pay-cheque."

"Of course. Here I am talking about being self-employed, and you already are. You like it?"

"It's hard, sometimes, but I'm living the life I want to live. I would not give it up for anything. Or anyone."

Dylan wondered if that was directed at him.

"You mentioned plans to become self-employed. What sort of business? Or can you do investment analysis as a self-employed consultant?"

"I'm considering some options." But he didn't want to talk about that, since the key was the money from the campground deal. "How do you find time for everything? Running the campground, marketing it, building facilities, cleaning them, preserving food, baking bread?"

"I like keeping busy. It helps that the campground is seasonal. Things are busy July and August, but other months are quieter, and there's little to do in the winter."

"You don't get lonely?"

"No. And there's always Cerebus. I can go into Bay St. Lawrence or down the trail if I want company."

As the sky darkened, they did not talk, or look at each other, but Dylan was aware of her presence. There was no wind, and the waves barely broke on the beach. He could hear the slight rustles of fabric as she brought her wineglass to her lips and sipped. He imagined kissing her, her lips still wet from the wine. It was a clear night, moonless, and the stars were at their most visible and spectacular, though Dylan imagined there was some haze on the horizon. He rubbed his eyes.

"There. Did you see it?" Marianna pointed to the horizon. "The green."

"Yes. What is it? Pollution?"

"Northern lights. I haven't seen them since I was here in my teens."

"I've never seen them. The haze? That's the northern lights?"

"Yes. If we're lucky, they'll get brighter."

The shimmer of green at the horizon widened, streaked upward, then faded. It grew again, looking like a reflection of the ocean. The colour shifted to shades of pink, and back to green, and waves of green rippled across the sky.

"Wow," whispered Dylan. "Like flames, but no heat or noise. I never expected it would be so, so silent."

"They do make a sound, but you can't always hear it over the surf."

They watched the display. "How long do they last?" asked Dylan.

"Anything from ten minutes to several hours. We're lucky to see them at all this time of the year, let alone so clearly."

Dylan was starting to feel the cold when the display faded, and he was torn between thinking they had ended too soon and looking forward to being inside and warmer.

Marianna stood up. "It was lovely, but if it had gone on much longer, I would have needed to go in for a blanket. Time for me to tuck in for the night. Thanks again for finding Cerebus." She picked up the wine bottle and checked the contents. "More?"

"No, thanks. I should head in, too." Dylan stood and picked up the dishes. Marianna called Cerebus, and Dylan followed them inside. He headed for the sink. "I'll take care of these."

"Not really fair, since you helped make the dinner. And I'm still worried about the review you will leave: 'One star. Made to do the dishes'." She followed him to the sink. "Let me get some water to heat up." She carried a filled pot to the stove.

"Five stars. After my car and tent were washed away by a flood, I was sent on a death march, forced to find a missing dog in treacherous woods, and dunked in a freezing ocean. Never had so much fun."

"I like the five stars, but not sure that write-up will encourage visitors. I'm going to take Cerebus out. We'll be right back. Can you put fresh water in his bowl, please? From the jug, not the pump, thanks."

Dylan dumped the dog's water bowl and filled it with fresh water. He was leaving tomorrow, he still hadn't figured out how to save the campground, and he did not know what to do about his feelings for Marianna. He knew he wanted to kiss her, even though there were so many sensible reasons not to. He pumped some water into the sink, added the warm water from the stove, and washed the dishes. Marianna came back inside, carrying Cerebus, and put him in his bed. Then she banked the fire in the stove. Dylan could see her reflection in the window. "I meant it," he said. "I've never had so much fun." He put the last dish into the rack and drained the sink.

Marianna closed the stove door and walked over to him. "Really?"

Dylan took her hands in his. "Tonight, I enjoyed dinner

under the stars, with a beautiful, hardworking, intelligent person." He leaned forward to kiss her.

She pulled back but did not let go.

"No?"

"I'm not sure ...."

"Neither am I. But remember what you said earlier? That we should listen to what our bodies tell us?"

* * *

"Yes. We should." She squeezed his hands, leaned forward, and kissed him. Dropping his hands, she grabbed his shoulders to pull him closer and pressed against him. He ran his hands up her back, making her tremble, as she lowered her hands to his waist. She could feel hesitation at his lips, but she could also feel him thickening against her belly, and then his hesitation faded. He pressed his mouth against hers, running his tongue over her lips, then broke off and kissed her throat, softly sucking. She lowered her hands to his butt—as firm as she'd expected—and ground against him. He kissed one ear, top and lobe, then the other, then returned to her mouth. He pulled one hand forward, around her side, and slid it between them to cup her breast. She shivered as his hand brushed her nipple, straining against the fabric. She wanted his hands on her, not her clothes.

She stepped back, enjoying his hungry stare, and pulled her T-shirt over her head, tossing it on the floor.

"Beautiful," he said.

"The lacy bra, or me?" She tried to sound indignant, but it came out husky.

He didn't speak, but moved forward, kissing her again on her mouth, neck, and between her breasts. She ran her hands over his back, feeling the smooth muscles twitch as he undid her bra strap. With his fingers spread wide, he slid his hands under the bra and around her, moving his hands forward until they were cupping both breasts. He ran his thumbs over her nipples. Heat spread from her breasts to her fingers, but his skin still felt hot to the touch.

She nibbled his lips. He gasped and pulled back, and she wondered if she'd bitten too hard, but he bent down, pressed his open mouth hard against her breast, and flicked her nipple with his tongue. Marianna felt her knees weakening. "Come on," she said, pulling back, taking his hand, and leading him out of the kitchen.

"I want you, but—."

"You said you were single. Will you wear a condom?"

"I am, and I will."

"We're good. I want you."

17

⌒

Chapter 17

Marianna woke early and wondered what had disturbed her. Cerebus wheezed in his bed beside the door. She recalled him barking at some point during the night, and Dylan bringing him up. There was a clump of sheets and blankets between her and Dylan. He was sleeping on his stomach and fully exposed. She rearranged the sheets to cover him, then stroked her hands down his back, over his butt, and down his legs, molding the sheets to his shape. He didn't respond. No wonder, she thought. The first time, they'd been eager, almost frantic, as if trying to make up for days of thinking about each other. He was a caring and thorough lover, especially the second or third time, depending how you counted things, somewhere in the middle of the night.

The night had been more intense than any of the few nights she'd welcomed a campground guest into her bed. Perhaps because we know each other, she thought, though she realized she still knew little about him. I don't even know his job or employer, she thought. She had known Troy well, but his lovemaking had always had a mechanical, methodical quality to it, as if he was marking steps on a list. Troy took the time to make sure she was satisfied, something she had appreciated, but now she knew he had lacked passion. Her satisfaction had been a duty. The difference last night was passion. It excited Dylan to see her pleasure, and that increased her pleasure. She lay on her side, and rested a palm against his side, feeling him breathe. *Where do I go from here?*

When she awoke again, it was full day, and Dylan snuggled against her back, one arm across her belly. She extricated herself, slid into a T-shirt and sweatpants, and went to the bathroom. While she brushed her teeth, she counted the hickeys on her neck and chest. Worth it, she thought.

When she came back from the bathroom, he was awake. "Good morning," he said. "Sleep okay?"

"Yes." She could play it cool. "You?"

He sat up and kissed her.

She steadied herself with her hands on his shoulders. I could get right back into bed, she thought. But I shouldn't. "I should take care of Cerebus. He must need out."

"Need help?"

"We should be fine." Marianna assisted Cerebus down to the main floor, stepping in front and slowing him. The porch stairs were easier. Once they were outside, Marianna started the generator, to cool the fridge and freezer. She brought Cerebus in and fed him. While he ate, she went to the office to check in with Mike on the radio.

"Yes, Gerry will out today. Around four, I expect."

"That'll be great, Mike. Thanks." It's for the best, she told herself.

"Frank can take him down to Baddeck, though he'll have to pay for dat."

In more ways than one, thought Marianna.

"Oh, and I have a message for you, from Grace." Grace was an elderly lady from Canso. She'd come to the campground last year with her daughter and grandchildren, all from Ottawa. Grace reminded Marianna of her grandmother, and they'd become friends, exchanging cards and occasional emails. "Grace's nephew, Dougie's oldest boy, lives down in Truro. He married a Swinton, remember?"

Marianna had no idea who Dougie or the Swintons were but said nothing. Mike would get to the point in his own time.

"Anyway, the nephew works at the car rental at the airport. Halifax. He says to Grace last week that he rented this big fancy SUV to some yakky city boy from Toronto. The guy worked for a finance company. Said he was coming up to Cape Breton to repossess some worthless campground in the middle of nowhere, somewhere's up past the Cabot Trail—his words, Grace said her nephew said—and turn it into luxury condos. Big real estate deal. Big project, all possible because of a scam loan he arranged. Well, the nephew, he remember Grace saying she liked your campground, so he told her because he figured it might be the place. She was going to call, but, like you said, your phone is gone. So, she ask me to tell you, just in case he come by your place. If you see some bastard who looks like he works in an office, just show him the boot. City people. What a sin. You haven't had anyone like that come by, have you?" He waited for her reply. "Big red SUV. Can't miss it." Static crackled. "Marianna? You still there?"

"I'm still here." Marianna gripped the arm of the old office chair. "Got to go. Thanks for the heads-up."

"No problem and see you later." Marianna heard the sink running in the kitchen.

* * *

Dylan went to his room to find some clothes, then returned to the bedroom, gathered the condoms and wrappers, and disposed of them in the bathroom garbage can. He considered making the bed and decided against it. It was her space. I'm not sure what the one-night stand etiquette is, he thought. But that wasn't really a one-night stand, or was it? It didn't feel like a one-night stand. It felt like something worth giving up Toronto and moving here for. Now that was a ridiculous idea. I'm thinking with my cock now. Still ... but they both knew he was leaving today, and she liked her life as it was. Last night would not be repeated but would never be forgotten. The least he could do was fix the deal with her campground, even if it cost him his job. And he should tell her everything. She deserved that. He'd tell her as soon as he'd worked it out. He'd woken with a few ideas. As soon as he could get online, he could confirm details and set things up.

He walked downstairs to heat some water on the stove, and shave. Cerebus was in the kitchen, eating, and the fire was roaring in the stove. A pot of water steamed. Marianna was not there. He heard the generator running, assumed she was outside, and started shaving.

"Who are you?"

Dylan looked up from the sink. Marianna was standing in

the doorway to the living room, arms pressed against the doorframe.

"Who are you, and what the hell are you doing here?"

"What happened?" Dylan put the razor down and wiped shaving soap off his face. She doesn't have a phone, he thought. How could she have learned anything?

She marched across the room and stood in front of him. "Do you work for the finance company that holds my mortgage?"

"Marianna, I—."

"Answer the damn question! Yes or no!"

Dylan shrank back, leaning against the counter. He could not meet her eyes.

"Yes."

"Did you come here to take the campground?"

"It's complicated. Let me explain."

"No. Get out. Go." She pointed her arm to the door. Cerebus stood up. He growled.

Dylan wanted to try to explain, though he was not sure he could, and he did not want to upset her further. She trembled with rage. Give her some time, he told himself. He picked up his shirt, walked out the porch, and onto the deck. The chairs were in the sun, but he could see her staring at him through the window. He walked down the stairs to the ground and hesitated. Where now?

He walked to the beach stairs, down to the beach, and settled at the picnic table on the rocky ledge where the lobster supper had been. The house was not visible from here. He'd run out of time. She knew at least some of the truth, and he wanted to tell her all of it, and the solution that redeemed him. He needed a solution. Now. He got up and paced.

First, he needed to work off tension. He did a set of push-ups, a set of sit-ups, and another set of push-ups. He'd been out of his morning routine for several days, and the occasional hike and swim was not a substitute. A swim would be a good workout, clear his head, and help him think. The waves were higher than last night, but still calm.

* * *

She saw him leave the deck and go down to the beach. He disappeared behind the bluff edge, then reappeared a few minutes later, heading for the water. "Good. Swim home. Drown, for all I care." She poured a mug of hot water for tea, spilling some on the counter, and sat down at the table. Cerebus trotted over, still favouring a leg, and rested his snout on her leg. She patted his head. "Thanks buddy. That's what I get for trusting a man, right?" She felt tears starting to come and fought them back. Stay angry, she thought to herself. And the friendliness, the inquiries about how the campground was doing, were just preparing his argument for seizing the campground. He's not worth being sad about. What else had he lied about? Probably everything, including the sister. Good riddance, she thought, and then remembered that he was stuck here until Gerry brought her boat this afternoon. But Dylan hadn't planned to stay. Maybe he still planned to seduce her but faster? He could not have planned or expected the washout. And he hadn't seduced her. She'd pursued him, even after he said he wasn't interested. Though he still acted interested. And she had not given him a chance to explain. Maybe Grace had misunderstood her nephew? But Dylan admitted working for the finance company and planning to seize the property. He hadn't actually lied about that, but he'd kept it a secret, which was almost the same.

Marianna paced the kitchen. Had the last few days all been an act? Was she that easily fooled? What did he want to explain, or was that part of the act? She started pacing again. I need to do something, she thought, and she heard her grandmother's voice. "Can't think on an empty stomach. Food first, worries second." She cooked a bowl of oatmeal, then started a loaf of bread, trying to punch out her anger with kneading. She glanced out the window a few times. No sign of Dylan. Did she need to make sure he was okay?

18

⌒⌒

Chapter 18

Two hours later, Marianna reviewed her progress on the picnic shelter. Anger had made her productive. She had cut and nailed up the plywood sheathing for one wall. She glanced towards the beach. Earlier, she'd left the house to check on him, just in time to see him stroll to the washrooms and back to the beach. He hadn't seen her, but it made her angrier to see him fine, and have her concern revealed as needless. Not that he was anything more than a customer at the campground, she told herself.

She put away the tools, calm enough to face him now. However much he'd misled her, she was running a business, and he was a customer. A difficult one. If he was with the finance company, he had power over her, and being angry with him would not help matters. And even prisoners got food.

She returned to the house and prepared a tray for him. Nothing fancy. A few slices of bread on a small plate, a jar of jam, cheese, one knife, one spoon, and a cup of tea. She brought it to the top of the stair. He was sitting at the picnic table. When she started down the stairs, he looked over, smiled, and stood up. She glared at him, and his smile vanished. Good. He had nothing to grin about.

She put the tray on the table, in front of him.

"Thanks. Will you sit for a moment? I'd like to talk."

Marianna sat down on the opposite bench of the table. She noticed Dylan held a spray of lavender sea rocket flowers in one hand. He placed the tiny flowers on the table in front of her. "Peace offering?"

"Flowers do not make it all better. I'm angry with you, but it was wrong of me to be angry based on what other people said, without giving you a chance to respond. So, I'm giving you that chance. But if even half of what I have learned about you is true, you are the most despicable person I have ever met."

"Please, sit down. Thanks for the tea." She sat down, and so did he. She waited for him to talk. Instead, he stared out over the ocean for several minutes.

"I told you I grew up poor. Worked my way up. I'm not poor anymore, but I'm still working for someone else. I told you I want to be self-employed. It's not because of not having a boss. The company I work for now is shady. The last couple have been like that." He looked down at the table. "The people I work for specialize in risky loans. Interest rates are high, and the collateral is always worth more than the loan. The way the loan agreement is worded, it's easy for us to claim a default, and seize the property." Dylan paused. "You're not going to like this next part."

"I don't like what I already heard."

"I'm not proud of my work, but the borrowers .... They're naïve, or overextended, or gambling, or trying to defraud us. At least, as far as I know. And the amounts were small. A few thousand, maybe a few hundred thousand. Nothing the borrower couldn't afford to lose. Until your campground. I don't know exactly what is going on, but there is a lot of money involved. My cut is enough for me to get out and get free of this."

"At the cost of stealing my campground. You came here to take it, didn't you?" Marianna stared at him. He looked up.

"Yes." He looked down, then over to the ocean, avoiding her eyes. "You knew your loan was a high risk and came with a number of conditions. One of them was that it could be called in at any time, and the property seized, if our inspection of the property and the business suggested you might miss future payments. They want your property, for a resort condominium development. It's a large private waterfront, it's exclusive, and it already has road access. Since it's already a tourist property, it does not require environmental assessments or farmland acreage removal hearings. Overseas investors are lined up, though I suspect nothing will be built, or it will be started and abandoned, like that property you showed me." Dylan rubbed his hands together.

"I researched your financial records and transactions and determined that you can't pay the loan if it's called. Most people can't. The only unknown was the chance you might have a rich friend or relative. I was pretty sure you didn't. I came out here to write the inspection report, all nice and legal, and it wasn't too hard to find evidence that I could put in the report, to claim you might miss payments."

"You bastard."

"Hang on—there's a happy ending to this, really." He looked up, and then away from her glare. "Being here, and being with you, I've found something that I didn't know I was missing. And I will not let it go. But I can't just quit and walk away from my job. That would not save your property. And there are clauses and conditions. If I don't complete the deal, they could sue me for everything I have, future earnings, and no financial company would hire me."

"If you're looking for sympathy from me," said Marianna, "forget it." There was no way she could feel sorry for him.

"But I found a way. I said there was a chance you might have a rich relative. You don't, do you?"

Marianna shook her head.

"You do. Your Great-uncle Robert died last week. He left you enough money to take over the mortgage."

"I don't have a Great-uncle Robert."

"He's not your uncle. That's just what you called him. He was a family friend, and you never knew his real name. That's why I didn't find him when I searched your relatives. You haven't seen him since you were a child, and then he moved to the Caribbean. But you always answered his letters, to whatever address he wrote from. You hadn't heard from him for six or seven years, but just recently you got a letter from a lawyer in Toronto, asking you to confirm your identity. Great-uncle Robert," Dylan drew air quotes when he said the name, "died, and he left you a substantial sum in a Cayman Islands bank account. His will said you were the daughter he never had, and he wanted to leave you his money. But he doesn't want to reveal his name. He wants you to focus on your future, not the past. Now you're just waiting for the Toronto lawyer to get the funds and send them to you. That's what I will say you told me. My mission to call in the loan will fail, since you will pay it out.

They'll fire me, as they need someone to blame, but I might get some severance, since it's not my fault you had a family friend to help."

"I'm receiving untraceable money? This is worse than dealing with a shady loan company. Where did the money come from? Is this some sort of money laundering thing?"

"No. Well, it might sound like money laundering, but everything is above board. I'll sell my condo. My reason for selling will be losing my job. Besides, I don't want it anymore. I can bridge finance the proceeds, to get the money to you before the sale goes through. The money won't go directly to you. That's to protect both of us. I'll give it to a lawyer I know in Toronto. She'll manage everything, and she'll contact you to transfer the funds." Dylan gave her a tentative smile. She did not return it. "I will save your campground by loaning you the money to pay off the loan."

"You'll hold the mortgage on my campground?"

"Not really. There won't be any mortgage. Just a simple promissory note with the terms. Unsecured. The monthly payment will be the same, but the penalties and seizure steps are gone. Your property will be yours, even if you have trouble making payments."

Marianna got up and walked around to his side of the picnic table. As horrifying as the story was, she understood Dylan was trying to switch from bad guy to good guy. Something was not right, though. "Why would you give me all that money? What's in it for you?"

"It's a loan, same as before. You'll pay me back, with fair interest, and I'll make money. It will be the first loan of my new company. Seeing the way you run this place, I know you are an excellent investment. And I'm doing the right thing. I'm investing, but not just for the money."

Marianna scoffed. "What happened to money being important to you?"

"It is, but so is doing the right thing. You made me see that. I love what you have created here. I love ... the place, and I love what you've done to make such a fabulous home and a growing business." He moved closer. She kept pacing. "You may not believe this, but I've learned a lot these past few days. I've realized I like being by the ocean. I'd forgotten that. I've done a lot of thinking, and I want to change not just how I make a living, but how I live. Where I live. I'm even thinking of moving out here. Leaving Toronto."

Marianna stopped pacing and stared at Dylan. He took her hands. She froze but did not pull her hands away. "You are a wonderful woman. I've never met anyone like you. You are ambitious, clever, smart, hardworking, gorgeous, and sexy. I know you expected our, our time here, to be temporary, right?" She was too angry to respond. "I don't want to push you into anything, but if I were to move out here, perhaps we could continue things, see where it goes?"

Marianna pulled free, walked to the foot of the stairs, and turned to face him. "FUCK YOU!" She took a step towards him, and he backed up. "You waltz in and save my campground, which is only in danger in the first place because of you." She moved closer. "Then you steal it, give me dirty money from some offshore account that will probably end up with me in trouble for tax fraud, and there's no strings except you want a relationship like I'm some cheap country mistress for you to fuck on Fridays because I'm so goddamned grateful for your rescue. What a sin!" She walked back to him and jabbed his chest with her finger. "I never want to see you again. I want you off my property as soon as possible. The boat's coming today, and if it doesn't, you can stay on the damn beach overnight."

"Marianna—I'm trying to do what's right, for you, for me, and for us."

"There is no us. Your pathetic idea about living here guarantees that. A city boy like you wouldn't last a week in the winters we get and don't expect me to believe you're all gaga over me after a few days. I ...." She didn't know what to say. "Goodbye!" She ran up the stairs and into the house without looking back.

* * *

Late that afternoon, she watched as Dylan met Gerry's dinghy. They talked for a moment, and Dylan shook his head. Gerry hopped out of the dingy, picked up a large plastic tub, and carried it up the stairs from the beach. Marianna met her at the porch. She put the tub down as Cerebus approached.

"Hey buddy." She petted the dog, then greeted Marianna. "How you been doing, then?"

"Good, thanks. Everything okay in town?"

"Oh yeah. Almost all cleaned up. They say your road should be fixed next week maybe. Janey's basement flooded, but that ain't no surprise. She and Susan got some stuff together for you they thought you might need." She lowered her voice and leaned closer, though no one was nearby. "So that feller give you any trouble? He seems worked up over something."

Marianna was tempted to say something that would ensure

Gerry, or even Mike and the boys, gave him what he deserved but decided on discretion.

"No, he's just annoyed. Lost his truck and all his gear when the road washed out."

"No shit."

"It was a rental, and he didn't have much gear, but even so. And then he's stuck here for a few days. Just ignore him. He's from Toronto."

"Ahh. Gotcha. We'll get him home, don't you worry."

Marianna watched from the deck as Gerry returned to the dinghy. She rowed it and Dylan out to the fishing boat. They climbed aboard, Gerry tied up the dingy, and a few minutes the boat roared away, leaving a cloud of diesel exhaust hovering above the waves.

Don't worry, she thought. I'm about to lose my home, the campground, everything, or owe everything to him. He'd been good company. She'd actually considered a relationship, difficult as it might be. But a relationship was impossible if she was in his debt. And he was a creep for thinking she owed him anything. Not that he'd said that, but it was obvious. The exhaust dissipated. I won't cry, she thought. Nothing to cry over. But the tears came anyway.

19

Chapter 19

Dylan appreciated that Gerry was a person of few words. He did not feel like talking. Once they climbed aboard the fishing boat, Gerry passed Dylan a life jacket. "Wear it. If you got to hurl or piss, do it over the side." She stepped into the small cabin and closed the door.

Dylan sat on a bench along the side of the boat. The diesel motor sputtered to life, and a cloud of smoke formed overhead before they headed away from the shore. Dylan looked back at the campground. He could see Marianna on the deck but did not wave. Neither did she.

He had screwed that up. The financial arrangements would go ahead, as he had promised. He trusted her to not contradict his statement to the company and use the funds to pay out the loan. And pay him back. Dylan was sure she would do that. However much she might not like his solution, it saved her campground and did not cost her anything. She could reject his deal and try fighting the seizure in court, but even if she succeeded, the court costs would wipe her out. She was angry with him, but too smart and practical to reject the deal he offered. It would be strictly business though. He'd screwed up the personal relationship. She was angry with him, both for being with the company that had been planning to steal her land, and for implying he expected any kind of reward for stopping that. He did not expect a reward. Stopping the seizure meant a relationship was possible, if she wanted one, but she'd misunderstood, and, thinking about what he had said, he could not blame her. After that, friendship was probably out of the question, let alone anything else he imagined might happen if he tried moving here.

As they entered the village harbour, Dylan surveyed the surrounding houses that climbed the hillsides. It was small, remote, and isolated, even compared to his memories of the south shore town he'd come from. But it looked urban after the campground.

They bumped against the wharf, and a man attached ropes to the boat. He had the same raven hair as Gerry, but instead of crew cut he was bald with a full beard. Gerry cut the motor and emerged from the cabin.

Dylan stood up, holding the side of the rocking boat. "What do I owe you?"

"Reckon sixty will cover the gas and time. That be cash." Dylan handed over the bills.

"Thank you."

"Frank, my brother here," she gestured at the man, "will take you down to Baddeck."

"Let's go, in the truck then."

Dylan looked around the wharf. There was a pickup truck

and a tow truck, both with rust holes and dents under grime. They were obviously abandoned.

"Where's the truck?"

"Right here, you dumb-fuck city boy." Frank opened the passenger door of the rusted pickup, and climbed in. He used the steering wheel to pull himself across the bench seat. "They don't have trucks in Torona?"

"Paying customer, Frank," said Gerry. "Mind your manners."

Dylan decided that what Frank lacked in manners, he made up for in good driving. The threadbare seat cover added nothing to the flattened cushion but compared to the exposed wooden seat on the bouncing boat, the truck ride was luxury. The road through the highlands included detours where washouts and slides left only one lane open, and they passed crews removing fallen trees and fixing downed wires. Dylan could see that it would be several days yet before the crews reached Marianna's remote spot. While driving, always with two hands on the wheel, and never over the speed limit, Frank described weather forecasters, road crews, linemen, and various government officials as dumb-fucks. After several hours of this, Dylan realized "dumb-fuck city boy" was a practically a term of endearment, coming from Frank.

Frank stopped at a bank machine, waited while Dylan withdrew cash, and grunted in appreciation when Dylan added twenty to the requested payment. "Anytime, buddy. For a dumb-fuck city boy, you're all right."

The car rental company had an agent at a local garage. Dylan was unsure what to expect when he reported the lost car, but the agent told him it was the third car destroyed during the storm. One had slid into a ditch, and another was flooded in a parking lot. The agent apologized for not having another SUV, but Dylan was happy with the compact car they provided. A drugstore next door sold basic cell phones, and Dylan bought last year's entry-level Samsung at a great price. Twenty minutes later, he was online, enjoying free Wi-Fi, scallop fettuccine, and a view of the Bras d'Or Lake from a restaurant's upper-level deck.

He caught up on emails and skimmed social media notifications. Then he composed a brief email to his company. He reported inspecting the property, discussing the matter with the owner, and that she laughed in his face when he announced he would call in the loan. "She expects to pay the loan out within a week, having just received money from a recently deceased family friend that I was not aware of." He apologized for the delay in reporting and provided a link to a CBC article about the storm damage to the area. Just before hitting send, he added that he would be returning later in the week, after visiting family in Nova Scotia. He needed to do that. He imagined the reactions to his email Monday morning, and wondered how long before Carla fired him. He booked his return flight and updated his car rental reservation. He wondered what it would take to have good internet at the campground. Not that it was any of his concern.

"Dessert, sir?"

"Perhaps." The sun was starting to set over the lake, and it was living up to its golden name. Dylan was happy to spend more time here. "What do you have?"

"There's a mess of pies, but on Saturday nights the best is the apple. Homemade today."

"Homemade?"

"Mom makes them at home, from our own apples. Tell you a secret, sir. The others come from Sobeys. But they're the store-baked ones, so still pretty good."

"I'll take the homemade apple."

The pie was as good as anything Dylan had tasted at high-end dessert bars in Toronto, and considerably cheaper. And nowhere in Toronto had a view like this. Harold, the waiter, recommended a local hotel on the lake, and answered Dylan's questions about living in the area. As the stars came out over the lake, Dylan remained at the table. It was beautiful, but not the same as over the ocean. With Marianna.

20

❧

Chapter 20

Dylan stayed another day in Baddeck, then left early Monday to visit his sister. He stopped in Antigonish for lunch and checked his email. As expected, he was fired, with a note apologizing for the lack of notice, but stating "Recent events have made it necessary to streamline our operations as quickly as possible." It was not fair, but he had never expected the company to be fair, and the severance offered was what he had expected.

He phoned the lawyer he'd emailed the day before. He knew she was eager for paying work, and she agreed the arrangement he proposed was legal, if unorthodox. "Half the requests I get are for straight-up money laundering, but this is a simple loan between individuals. You're not related, and the interest rate is reasonable. Whatever story the two of you tell the finance company about where the money came from, or why you want to keep this private, is nothing to do with me."

Dylan also contacted a real estate agent he knew. The agent assured him his condo would sell within days and offered to handle bridge financing to make the funds available immediately.

Midafternoon, Dylan turned onto Red Barn Lane, in Sandport, just outside Yarmouth. Mature trees shaded the street, and the large yards were well kept. The houses were modest raised ranches from the 1970s, but well-maintained and painted in a mix of bright colours. Several had bicycles or children's toys in the front yard, or basketball hoops in the driveway.

Dylan stopped on the street in front of number 42. He realized his plan to surprise them depended on them being home. A boy of about six ran out of the front door and around the house to the backyard. A younger girl chased him, shrieking. Dylan recognized Alison and Cole from photos Jennifer sent at Christmas. He got out of the car and started walking towards the house. The kids ran into the front yard from the other side of the house. They skidded to a halt when they saw Dylan. "Who are you?" Cole asked.

"I'm your Uncle Dylan. We've never met, though. It's good to see you."

"You sent me a nice ponies calendar at Christmas," said Cole.

"I'm glad you liked it. Thank you for remembering me and the gift."

"Thank you, sir."

"And very well mannered."

"Thank you, sir. This is my sister, Alison."

"Hi Alison. You look even cuter than in your pictures."

The girl looked at Dylan for a moment, then ran into the house, yelling "Mom! Cole's talking to a stranger!"

"It's Uncle Dylan!" yelled Cole through the screen door. "From Toronto." Cole turned to Dylan. "Mom Jennifer's home, but Mom Tina's at work."

"Pull the other one," yelled Jennifer from inside. But she came to the door and yanked it open. "My goodness. Dylan? Here? What's going on? Why didn't you call? Is everything okay?"

"Hi Jennifer, good to see you. Everything is fine."

* * *

"So, everything is not fine." Two hours later Dylan and Jennifer were sitting on the deck at the back of the house. Cole and Alison had lost interest in the visitor and were playing in a sandbox under a tree at the back of the yard.

"It's not that bad," said Dylan. So far everything was working as planned, though he appreciated why it seemed bad to Jennifer.

"Seems it is that bad," said Jennifer. "You've lost your job and your girlfriend, and you're in such a muddle you're interested in family again and slumming with your sister for the first time in over ten years. What's come over you?"

"Well, I ...." Dylan paused. He looked around the deck, noting that some boards needed replacing. An older minivan pulled alongside the house, and both kids ran towards it, yelling "Tina, Tina."

Jennifer stood up. "Tina's here. Mind your manners."

Dylan protested, but Jennifer was already halfway to the van. He followed. Jennifer had been friendly, if guarded, as he had told her about his days in Cape Breton, but she had not volunteered information about Tina, and Dylan hadn't asked.

Tina stepped out of the van and greeted Jennifer with a kiss. The family photos Jennifer emailed were posed Christmas portraits, and the kids at play. This was the first time he'd seen Tina and Jennifer looking relaxed and happy together. He felt a pang of envy as the kids hugged Tina.

Cole pointed out Dylan to Tina. "Look Mom! Uncle Dylan came to visit us."

Tina noticed Dylan for the first time. She glanced at Jennifer, still smiling, and stepped forward. Dylan offered his hand. "Good afternoon Tina. Nice to meet you."

"Go on with you, we're family." Tina gave him a hug, then stepped back. "My god, it's been, what, ten, twelve, years since I've seen you? Just a teenager then and look at you now. Jenni didn't say anything about you coming. Everything okay?"

"I surprised her. I hope it's okay."

"It's great. Delighted to see you. How long are you staying?"

"Just for the day. I have a motel for the night and I'm flying back to Toronto tomorrow. I don't want to impose."

"Nonsense! You're family, you won't be staying at a motel. The living room couch is a sofa bed. We'll sleep there, and you can have our room."

"I'm sure he'd rather sleep in a motel than here," said Jennifer. "More the luxury he's used to."

"Well," said Dylan, "if you're sure it's not an imposition, I'd rather stay with you. I have a lot of catching up to do with you and the children. But I can't take your bed. The couch will be fine—better than my tent." And cheaper, since I need to watch my spending, he thought. But not as nice as Marianna's bed.

"Then it's settled," said Tina. "I'm planning to barbeque burgers for dinner. You okay with that?"

"Sounds great. Anything I can do to help?"

"Can you chop onions?"

Jennifer was about to speak, but Dylan interrupted her. "Would you believe I've taken a class that included chopping onions?"

"I didn't know people needed classes for such things, but okay. Follow me." Tina headed into the gleaming kitchen, and Dylan followed. She set him up with a bag of onions, a knife, and a cutting board. "Small pieces. The entire bag. We'll fry'em, and whatever doesn't get used tonight will be ready for soup or sauces all week. I'll be right back. I need to change out of my work duds."

Dylan started cutting. Within minutes, Tina was back, having swapped her jeans and Yarmouth Mariners sweatshirt for a pale-yellow sundress. "You want a drink? I got beer, wine, pop."

"Thanks. I'll join you in a beer."

"I'm having wine," said Tina. "It's a middling Australian red. Very dry, which I like, but not everyone does."

"I'll try it, thanks."

Tina poured half glasses for herself and Dylan, then toasted, "To family."

"To family," repeated Dylan. Tina drank a sip, then set the glass down. She looked out the window. Jennifer was sitting on the deck, looking at something Cole and Alison had found in the yard. "You're family, so you're welcome here, and why you're here is your business. But you've caused Jenni a lot of grief over the years. I don't know exactly what it's about but let me be clear about something." Dylan stopped cutting and put the knife down. "If you are here to make amends, that's great.

If your being here is going to upset her, I won't stand for that. Do you understand me?"

"I do," replied Dylan. "I'm here to make amends."

"Excellent," said Tina. "Glad to hear it. Don't be all day with those onions." She put an apron, white with blue flowers, over her dress, then took a package of meat from the fridge, dumped it into a mixing bowl, and started adding spices. "Jenni can be stubborn sometimes. Is she responding to peace offers?"

"Not really. She accepted my apology, but then I asked her advice about something, and she chewed me out for things that are too late to change."

"That's a good sign. She'll come round. When I talked with her about leaving my job at the mill, she thought the idea absurd, but within a week she saw the benefits."

"You're not driving a forklift anymore?" asked Dylan.

"Goodness no. Well, sort of. I train people how to use forklifts and pallet trucks. You know what a pallet truck is?"

"Yes. They had one at the mall when I worked there. I remember getting a certificate to use it."

"Central Mall?"

Dylan nodded.

"Cool. You know the process. A little training, then a written test, then the practical. I travel to businesses all over, up to Halifax and through the valley."

"Your own business?" asked Dylan.

"No. I work for an outfit that rents equipment. I do the training, and I've been learning to do the repairs. But I'd like to go independent. I could provide mobile training and repairs. Places are keeping the machines longer than they used to, so they are breaking down more, but getting repairs done can take a long time, as there aren't many places that do it. The folks I work for aren't interesting in getting into training and service for equipment they don't own. I'm saving up to buy a cube van and equip it as a mobile shop for forklift and pallet truck repairs and maintenance."

"What about getting a bank loan? Or using the equity in the house?"

"There's not much equity in the house, and I won't risk what we own, in case interest rates go up. I tried to get a business loan, but the bank said my business plan was too risky. I also looked at government programs, but I'm too old for some of them, too young for others. You done with the onions?"

"Yes."

"Great. There's a lettuce in the fridge. If you could tear off a few leaves and wash them." Tina shaped hamburgers.

"Perhaps I could review your business plan? You know I work in finance, right?"

"Yes, Jennifer mentioned that. But from what she said I figured it was big corporate deals, not small business loans."

"Yes, but I got fired today."

"Well, that explains why you're bothering to visit us after all this time."

"I deserved that," said Dylan.

"Yep," said Tina. "I get that you're on the corporate fast track, or at least you were, but Jenni's missed you, and the kids don't know you at all. Still, at least you're here today."

"I should have come before." I should tell Marianna that I followed her advice, thought Dylan, but that's too personal, the way things are between us now. Yvonne never challenged me about Jennifer, he thought. He rinsed lettuce leaves under the tap. The shock of the cold water on his fingers brought him back to the present. "I'm starting my own financial business, focusing on helping small businesses. I can't promise anything, but I might be able to assist, or at least provide some suggestions for your business plan."

"Well, I'd appreciate that," said Tina. "We could chat after dinner and the kids are down, if that's okay."

"Of course. Can I ask you a personal question?"

"Who's the birth mother?"

"No, that's not my business, unless you want to share. I was wondering if you always make dinner. Do people really ask you who the birth mother is?"

"All the time. They want to know who the 'real mother' is. Bah. And they make guesses. When I'm dressed for work, they assume it's her." She gestured at the short sleeve of her dress, the only part visible under the apron. "When I'm dressed for home, they assume it's me. The kids tell people they have two real moms, Jennifer and Tina, and they're happy with that. Usually works for busybodies."

"So, no problems?"

"Oh, sometimes. But we're not so unenlightened here as you might think. Our Pride parade is nothing like Toronto's, but we have one."

"This place has changed a lot since I lived here."

Tina nodded. "Things are better than when I was young. As for dinner, it's usually me. Sometimes I work a late shift, or travel, so Jenni has to do everything. Only fair that I do as much as I can when I'm home. Just put the lettuce to drip-dry in the rack. There's a couple of tomatoes in the breadbox. Slice those, and we'll be ready to take everything outside."

Dylan watched Tina for a moment. She took a cast iron pan off a hook on the wall, splashed some olive oil into it, and added the onions. Dylan found it hard to believe a few minutes earlier she'd been acting like a sibling defending a sister from a sleazy date. The brother I should have been, thought Dylan. He understood why Jennifer was so attracted to Tina, and so defensive when Dylan had mocked her choice.

After dinner, Tina and the children did dishes, while Jennifer and Dylan chatted on the deck, about safe subjects like the children's school activities. Then Tina took the children for a walk. "Give you two a chance to talk about us," said Tina. The walk seemed a routine activity for the children.

"Does she always do this?" asked Dylan, as he waved goodbye.

"If she's home. She gets to chat with them, they all get some exercise, and I get some quiet time. It helps settle them for bed."

"Sorry to disrupt your quiet evening, Jennifer. I know you're not happy that I'm here."

"Dylan, I am thrilled you are. You're family, and it's great to see you. But, frankly, you've been a jerk for years. It hurts that you never bothered to visit before."

"I know, and I'm sorry. I did apologize."

"Yes, and thank you. That was appreciated, but it's still hard to forget everything."

"I'm hoping to make up for my past. In fact, Tina and I were talking, and I might be able to help her with the business she wants to start."

"Of course. You can solve any problem with money, right? Like your fling at the campground. You thought you could pay her off. No wonder she was pissed."

"It wasn't like that at all. I mean, she needed money. People do. But I wasn't trying to buy her."

"How do you think it seemed to her? Did you tell her how much she meant to you? Did you tell her your feelings about her? Did you tell her what the point of the money was? Or did you just drop a wad of cash and expect her to be grateful?"

The wind shifted, and Dylan caught a whiff of salt air. He remembered watching the sun setting over the ocean. "I led with the money. I thought that was the main concern. I think that was a mistake."

"Damn right it was. Money's important, we all know that. But so is respecting people, especially if you are loaning them money. No matter what the situation, people don't enjoy needing money or borrowing money. They already feel low. Unless you treat them well, they'll figure out some way to avoid taking your money. But you can't treat people well, because you don't respect people, just money. You've always been like that, and you're too stubborn to change. Marianna saw that and didn't want your money. She'll take it, because from what you said, she's smart, but she won't be happy about it. I know how you feel about Tina, and with that attitude there's no way she'll take your money."

The yard looked over grain fields, and the sun was setting behind a barn in the distance. Dylan watched the sun sink lower, composing his thoughts. Jennifer was right, but he could change. Hadn't he changed already? Or at least started? He wasn't sure. He wanted to defend himself.

"Money's important. Don't you remember how poor we were when we grew up? How Dad was always broke? How our parents fought about money?"

"We grew up no worse than a lot of other people, and better than most. You used to compare yourself to the richest kids in the school. I know you worked long hours after classes, but what about the kids who worked instead of going to school? Or the kids that ran away and lived on the street in Halifax because their parents beat them, or sexually abused them? Remember Candace? Pregnant by her uncle?" Dylan remembered Jennifer being friends with a pregnant girl, and her coming over to the house sometimes, but didn't recall the details. "Our childhood wasn't perfect, but our parents did a decent job. They weren't perfect either, but people aren't. That's okay."

"If they'd had more money—."

"Dad would have worried about something else. They would have found something else to fight over. If you've got to find fault with our parents, it was that they foolishly argued about money, not that they did not have enough. And you're going down the same road. How many emails do I get saying you'll come next year, after you get a better job, or get a bonus? But it's never enough, is it?"

Dylan bit his tongue on his response and absorbed Jennifer's words. The yard was completely in shade now. Dylan looked up. Not as many stars as in Cape Breton, but more than Toronto.

"I'll be back in a minute." Jennifer went into the house.

Dylan got up and strolled to the end of the backyard. He leaned on the fence, looking back at Jennifer and Tina's house. Between the houses across the street, he could see the ocean. I wonder if Marianna is looking at the same ocean, he thought. He heard the screen door slam as Jennifer came back outside. I am changing, he reminded himself. I still have a long way to go.

"Dylan?"

He walked back to the deck. "Jennifer, first, I owe you another apology. I was completely wrong about Tina. I assumed she was something she's not. She's wonderful and obviously cares about you a lot. In fact, she threatened me if I upset you. So, if she comes home now and sees you looking flustered, I'm a dead man. Second, you are just as stubborn as I am. Must be a family trait. I'm here, I'm asking your advice, I'm apologizing to you, because I have changed. I don't know exactly how it happened, but it was something to do with Marianna. I'm a better person after my time with her. So, you need to stop being so stubborn and see that."

"Tina told you I was stubborn, did she?"

"Yes, but I can see that for myself. Takes one to know one."

"Family's one thing. We're always together, like it or not, so I can wait around for years to hear you admit you've been a jerk. Let me savour this for a moment."

"Did I admit that?"

"Yes." She grinned and sipped her wine. "As for Marianna, treat her with respect for a while. As a person, not a financial problem. Show her you can do that. You might not win her back, but at least if someone else comes along you'll be ready."

The children came running into the yard.

"We saw a bunny!"

"I got pictures!" Cole waved his phone. Dylan and Jennifer leaned forward as he showed a set of pictures of the large brown hare. "His ears and feet are white. He's two colours."

"He is now," said Tina, "but he's turning white for winter."

"How does he know it's winter?"

"It's getting colder, and the days are getting shorter. It's already dark, which means time for bed. Come on, you two. Say good night to your Uncle Dylan."

"Uncle Dylan, will you be here tomorrow?"

"Yes, but I'll be leaving after breakfast."

"Will you come and visit again?"

"Yes, I will, Cole."

"Will you be back for Halloween? I'll be going as Bardunminko!"

"No, not that soon, sorry." I may not know much about kids, he thought, but that disappointment is easy to recognize. "Please send me a picture of your costume, okay?" Cole nodded. "I'd love to see your ... what are you going as?"

"Bardunminko!"

"Bardunminko," repeated Dylan. Whatever that was. "Soon I'll be living closer, and visiting you more often. I don't exactly when yet, but maybe by Christmas."

"Cool. Good night, Uncle Dylan." Alison mumbled a good night. Dylan wondered if he was supposed to hug them, or if Tina would suggest that, but she shepherded them inside.

Dylan looked past the children at the dark field. He'd taken steps to end his old life. Being closer to family was a step to starting his new life. But one visit was not closer. He needed to do more.

21

◈

Chapter 21

Marianna heard a truck approaching. Road must be fixed, she thought. She stood up, stretched, and looked down at the gate from the nearly completed picnic shelter. A New Brunswick Highways truck drove through the open campground gate. The government must have requested out-of-province help. She waved at the driver. Moments ago, she had nailed the last section of wall sheathing in place. With a week of fine weather, no power, no internet, and no guests, she'd had lots of time to work on the shelter. Pounding nails and hand-sawing wood felt good. Still, she'd appreciate not having to haul buckets of hot water up the stairs for her bath tonight.

The truck stopped next to the shelter. Cerebus trotted over. The driver cracked the door, saw Cerebus and shut it. He rolled the window down. "Road is fixed. You been doing okay out here?"

"All good, thanks. What's the word on power?"

"Nova Scotia Power is there now, so back on any minute. Bell is there too, so you should get your cell service soon.

There's some other problem with the landline though. That might take longer."

"I don't have landline service. The wire was down when I moved here, and it would cost a lot to fix. I just use the cell service." And I need to buy a new phone, she thought. She'd heard from Mike that police had checked the wreck. They had not found anything in the truck. Dylan's clothing and gear had washed out to sea. Even if they had found her phone, in one piece, it would be ruined by the water. She'd be able to go online with her laptop. Maybe there'd be a message from Dylan. Marianna was not sure if she wanted one, and if she did, whether she wanted an apology or an explanation. Maybe there'd be something from the finance company.

"Cerebus! Come here! Let him go." She waved at the driver. "Thanks."

As the truck drove away, she saw the outside light come on at the house. She ran towards the house. "I so need a long, hot shower," she said to Cerebus, who ran alongside her. "No sign of a limp. Who's a lucky, healthy dog?" Marianna glanced at the beach stairs, remembering Dylan appearing there with an injured Cerebus. "He was just doing his job," she reminded herself. "It was business. Nothing personal."

* * *

Showered, warm, and wrapped in a terry bathrobe, Marianna reviewed the lengthy list of emails that had downloaded while she had been in the shower. Nothing from Dylan, or the finance company. However, there was an email from a lawyer in Toronto, asking her to electronically sign several forms to receive a loan. The amount was enough to cover the total due the finance company, and a thousand extra. He'd gone ahead with his plan, without her agreement. She could still refuse, which would cause trouble for him, but that would be cutting off her nose to spite her face. She could at least get a lawyer to review everything or try to find other financing. But she knew her credit rating was poor, and, though she did not want to, she still trusted Dylan, at least with business issues. The promissory note was short and simple, as he had promised. She replied, agreeing to the terms.

Several people had emailed to ask if she was okay after the storm, including her mother. Marianna posted quick updates to the campground social media accounts, ordered a new alternator for her truck, then used Skype to phone her mother.

"Yes?"

"Hi Mum. I'm fine."

"So glad to hear from you at last. I wasn't worried at first, since you've had lots of storms there, and I know you are sometimes without power or internet, but it's been over a week. I tried calling your fisherman friend, but his phone wasn't working either."

"The rains washed out the road to the campground, and took down some power lines, but it's all fixed now. How are you doing?"

"The road washed out? Any campers stranded there?"

"No. Well, one. You're never going to believe who this guy was." Marianna related the visit of Dylan, leaving out a few details she was not interested in sharing with her mother, but her mother picked up on something in her voice.

"You liked him, despite why he was there?"

"Yes. Until I learned he was only interested in the campground."

"It sounds like he was interested in you too, especially with the deal he made."

"He lied to me. That's hardly an auspicious foundation for a relationship. And now he expects me to date him because he loaned me money."

"Did he actually say that?"

"He hoped we could still get together. I know what that means. But I can't have a relationship with someone when I owe them money. It could never work."

"Are you sure about that? It sounds like he trusted you enough to loan you the money with very few conditions. What would happen if you didn't pay?"

"I don't know. He could sue me, I suppose, though that would be costly, and he knows I don't have anything except the campground. And the land isn't worth what I borrowed to set up the campground."

"So, he's unlikely to sue, and you own the campground free and clear. If it wasn't for the money, would you want to be with him?"

Marianna thought about the evenings in the kitchen, washing dishes. Being at the beach. Spending the night together. "Maybe. But that doesn't change the fact that he lied. His talk about wanting to move here might be a lie too. How can I have a relationship with someone who lies like that?" She recalled her grandmother's letter. Had her mother lied to her about her father?

"You know the advice I give: don't expect men to be perfect."

"I know Mum. You said that about Troy, but this is hardly the same situation. I barely know the guy, and what I found out as I got to know him was that he was a complete slimeball. Like Troy."

"But you said he apologized, which, if memory serves, Troy never did. And he tried to fix the mess he made. Maybe he's a decent fellow, on the whole."

"It doesn't matter, Mum. I'm better on my own. I've known enough men to know that. And look at Dad. He walked out on you and me, right?" She tried not to overemphasize the question.

Her mother grunted.

"He walked out, right? That's what you always said. Though Grandma never said it." Marianna waited, listening to static and echoes on the line.

"Marianna, there's something I need to tell you." Her mother's voice took on a strained tone Marianna had not heard before.

"It's about your father." Marianna leaned forward in her chair, relieved. It had taken little to get her mother talking. "Your father and I had a complicated relationship. He wasn't perfect. No one is, of course. We'd been married several years, and things ... things weren't working out. We talked, got counselling. Finally, one day, after our biggest, and last, argument, he told me that he was, well, he didn't use the word, but he was gay. It was something he struggled with. Back then people weren't open about it like they are now, and his family was very conservative. He had told me he was an orphan, but he'd lied about that. He was estranged from his family. Never did tell me who they were. He'd married me to try to go straight, and it wasn't working. He loved me, and I loved him, we agreed on having children, but he was blocking out a part of himself, and that was bad for both of us. We talked, and we made an arrangement."

Marianna wondered what this arrangement entailed and decided she did not want to know.

"After that, things were much better. For us, at least. My mother, your grandmother, told me I should leave him. She had some old-fashioned ideas. We quarrelled. After that, my mother and I were always civil, but distant."

Marianna tried to imagine her always pleasant grandmother as an intolerant or bitter woman. Her mother seemed to be waiting for her to say something.

"I'm sorry."

"I hoped we would work things out, eventually. Perhaps if she had met him and understood how her beliefs hurt people. She was a free spirit, especially after your grandfather died, and yet she was so prejudiced against your father, and our love for each other. I've tried to raise you free of prejudice, and you get your free-spirited nature from her. It's a powerful combination, though I had my doubts when you were in high school. I wasn't as easily fooled as you thought."

Marianna recalled a few dates where she'd lied to her mother about the dinner enjoyed or the movie seen, or both.

Her mother continued. "I guess I was a free spirit in my own way, but Russell was my only love. And then he died."

Marianna gasped. She'd never considered trying to meet her father, but in the back of her mind it was always an option. The letter had made her wonder, but her mother's word made it clear. He was dead and she would never see him. Her mother kept talking, and Marianna tried to put her own grief aside and pay attention to her mother.

"He had HIV. Back then it was called AIDS, and they didn't have the drugs we have now. I was four months pregnant with you when he was diagnosed, and he died before you were born. His life insurance refused to pay, and the landlord gave me a month to get out of our apartment. There was a lot of prejudice around AIDS. We lived in St. Thomas then, but it was everywhere. Your dad worked at the auto plant. It was a small town, and somehow almost everyone knew. Grocery clerks would close their lane when they saw me coming. There were nasty rumours about our lifestyle. I tried to get an apartment in London, but people either assumed I was on welfare or a widow with a big life insurance payment. One guy said I'd have to sleep with him to get the place, but that shouldn't bother me since I was a single mother. I'd lost my love and was going through hell."

"I'm sorry. I had no idea."

"I decided being a single mother would be easier in a bigger city, and craved the anonymity, so I moved to Toronto. And, Goddess help me, I told everyone my husband had abandoned me when I got pregnant. As a widow of a gay man, I'd been shunned. As a widow, I was assumed wealthy. As an abandoned woman, I got sympathy and support. I'm not proud of what I did, but it's what I had to do, for us. At least, it's what I thought I had to do at the time."

"Why did you lie to me?"

"I always meant to tell you when you were older, but every year it got harder. I kept putting it off. I know it made you leery of relationships. Then you met Troy, and I figured you'd be okay. That didn't work out, and now I'm wondering if you're too cautious to trust when a good one comes along. I'm sorry I lied to you. It wasn't fair to Russell, or you, but I know he would have understood. He was a wonderful man. I hope you can forgive me for not telling you sooner."

Over the next few weeks, Marianna had several long phone calls with her mother, learning about her father. Now that her mother was no longer keeping the secret, she was bursting to share and reminisce, including their brief and rocky courtship.

"I can't believe you decided to marry him the day you met him," said Marianna.

"It just seemed right. I trusted my feelings, even though I hardly knew him. I've no regrets, despite everything. That's why I think you should give this Dylan another chance."

"Even if we were suited, which we are not, he's gone back to Toronto," Marianna said.

"He offered to move to Nova Scotia. He's from there. Makes sense that he'd go back."

"You never did," said Marianna. "Maybe he's like you?"

"I never doubted being here. The bigger the city, the happier I am."

"Well, he hasn't said anything, and it's not like he hasn't had the chance. I've got to go. Cerebus needs out." She ended the call, then checked email and social media. Nothing from Dylan, of course, but he'd liked a photo she'd posted on the campground Facebook page a few days ago.

"Come on, Cerebus! It's only snow." Though it was tiny stinging flakes, blowing sideways in the north wind. Cerebus looked at the open door from his bed, shook his head, and settled back into his bed by the stove. Marianna, holding the door open, tried again. "Cerebus! Outside! Now! Pee before bed!" The dog stood, stretched, and ambled out the doors. Marianna waited, closing the door against the wind and watching Cerebus. The whirling snow, glaring white under the porch light, went dark. Marianna did not need to look back into the kitchen to know the power was out. This was the first outage since Dylan's visit. First outage this winter, she corrected herself.

She wished she had given him more of a chance to apologize. He had tried to make things right, and she had refused to see that. But now he was back in Toronto, and she'd never see him again. One day her pulse wouldn't quicken when she got an email or a Facebook like from him, because it was just business, and no feelings involved.

Dylan was far from perfect, and he'd lied about why he came, but he'd been honest at the end. It had occurred to Marianna, when she paid out the loan, that she only had Dylan's word the finance company wanted to call the loan and seize the property, or that he'd be fired if the loan did not get called. However, when she had phoned to pay the loan out, the receptionist told her Dylan was no longer with the company. The receptionist connected Marianna to Carla, who said she'd been expecting Marianna's call.

Carla had threatened to sue Marianna for violating the terms of the loan by not supplying all her income and asset information when she applied, but Marianna had remained firm that it was accurate at the time, and that the loan did allow for early repayment. Carla had backed down but insisted on an early repayment penalty fee of five hundred dollars. Marianna recalled the extra thousand Dylan had arranged and assumed he'd been expecting there would be an extra fee.

Cerebus did not stay outside any longer than necessary. He slipped back in, and they walked through the dark kitchen and up the stairs to her room. It was warm, but if the power was out all night, it would be chilly in the morning. She put an extra quilt on the bed and settled in.

There'd been no power the night she'd gone to bed with Dylan .... He emailed once a month to thank her for her loan payment. She knew from LinkedIn that he was working at a new finance company, in Toronto. It was probably his own since he seemed to be the only employee. He'd started up the business he wanted. He had done okay. Not that she wasted time looking him up online.

In the morning, the power was back, and the snow was melting. She wrote holiday cards for all her guests from the past year and the year before. For Dylan, she hesitated over the note. "Hope you enjoyed your stay" did not seem appropriate. "Thanks for stealing my heart?" Too bitter. Maybe it would work on a child's valentine, complete with a picture of a masked robber. She settled on "Cerebus says hi." She wondered if she'd get a card from him, since she was his customer, however much she had not wanted to be.

A few weeks later, days before Christmas, she received a holiday card from his business. He'd written "Really enjoyed my visit!" The date mailed suggested he'd waited to hear from her before sending his card.

Then, early in January, she received a package from a used bookstore in the United States. It contained two books, by Henry De Vere Stacpoole: *The Garden of God* and *The Gates of Morning*. The enclosed note read "Merry Christmas from Dylan to Marianna. Hope you enjoy these sequels to *The Blue*

Lagoon." She checked the date, and the books had been mailed before she mailed her card to Dylan. Marianna had not known there were sequels. She read them both during a snowstorm that extended several days. The stories were disappointing, but she emailed Dylan thanking him for his thoughtfulness. She received a curt "you're welcome" in return. Maybe all his customers got books?

After the package at Christmas, she'd wondered if he might make some romantic gesture on Valentine's Day, but it came and went as usual: her and Cerebus watching *Groundhog Day* and sharing a pizza. The following day, she received an email from the Toronto lawyer who had set up the promissory note. Though it was short and simple, she read it three times, trying to figure out what it meant.

Please be advised that, effective March 1, your note is held by 902555 Canada Inc, and all payments should be made to that company. They will contact you to provide payment details. No other conditions have changed.

She called the lawyer and confirmed that this company was unrelated to Dylan. It seemed he had sold the loan to a small finance company in Alberta. The lawyer confirmed that none of the conditions of the loan had changed but could not provide other details about the sale. Marianna ended the call assuming Dylan wanted nothing further to do with her, and by selling the loan he had ended all connections between them. So much for her speculation about the books at Christmas. He wanted nothing to do with her. I won't see him again, she thought, and tried to convince herself that was for the best.

22

⌇

Chapter 22

The day was sunny, though cold, and the roads were clear, but there was snow in the forecast, and the locals warned Dylan that March could be deceiving. Taking their advice, he'd booked a hotel in Sydney for the night, though it was only an hour away. The trip included driving over Kellys Mountain, and the steep slopes could be hazardous in the winter. As he passed the St. Ann's turnoff to the Cabot Trail, at the base of the mountain, a sign with flashing lights warned of high winds ahead.

Dylan could not drive past the turnoff without thinking about Marianna and her campground at the tip of the island. He drove by every time he went to Sydney, which had turned out to be less often than he expected, thanks to online deliveries and the village stores. It helped that he was living in a motel, and the family that ran the place took care of most meals. Having his meals cooked and his linens cleaned had seemed a needless luxury, but his business had grown faster than expected and he often worked long hours. The Toronto-based company he'd established was producing a steady income on several loans, including Marianna's until he sold that loan, and the local shingle he'd hung out had attracted more clients than he'd expected.

Life in Baddeck was a big change from Toronto, but better in every way. His morning run was in fresher air, and even during the day the village streets were quiet, with enjoyable walks. The locals had warned him it would be busy in the summer, and the main highway in front of the motel was busy after the Newfoundland ferry came in, but even then, he could enjoy the view of the Bras d'Or Lake and the hills beyond from his efficiency suite. The winter had been harsh, but on the worst days he stayed in. No office meant no commuting.

Today he was driving to Sydney to give a talk on taxes for small business owners, at the public library. With any luck, he'd drum up some new customers, or at least meet some local people. He worked with existing customers online, when and where it was convenient for them, but he preferred to build his business meeting people in person. Loaning people money, and telling them what to do with the money they had, required trust. That was easier to create in person.

He hadn't told Marianna he'd moved. She'd been angry with him, and she had every right to be. But she'd accepted the money, paid out the finance company loan, and made the monthly payments to him. She must have understood he had helped, but he didn't want to tell her that. She'd sent him a holiday card, since he was a customer, and he'd sent one to her, though the wording had been difficult. "Thank you for your business," seemed inappropriate since she had not chosen to borrow from him. Not that she had any choice. Her credit rating was too low for anyone other than predatory lenders. But he was doing well by loaning to people the banks wouldn't touch, at better rates than the predatory lenders.

The views from Kellys Mountain always impressed him, and he wondered if he'd ever tire of the sight. The northern part of Nova Scotia was much more scenic than the south, though he'd made that trip several times since moving here. He'd helped Tina get her business going, including financing the truck and tools, and her list of customers was growing. Jennifer teased that Dylan was to blame for Tina being away overnight more often but appreciated the higher income she was making, and Dylan's help towards her goals.

When he visited last weekend, Jennifer had asked how things were going with Marianna.

"I'd like to contact her, let her know I'm here and would like to see her, but it might be too soon. I sold the loan to someone else and kept the terms the same to be fair to her. But she might think that I think she still owes me for making the loan in the first place, or for keeping the same terms when I sold it. And she hasn't contacted me. Maybe I'll tell her I've moved after the winter is over."

What he really wanted to tell her was that the world was a better place because of her, and even if he never saw her again, he would love her always. His time with her would always be a highlight of his life. He'd changed because of her. He wanted her to know this. It was simpler than that—he wanted her. He couldn't tell her any of this by email. It had to be in person. But he kept delaying asking to see her, in case she said no, or dismissed their time as a simple fling, or just wasn't interested in being with someone.

* * *

It was her first drive south of the village this year. Cabin fever had not set in, and Marianna loved the solitude of the campground in winter, but the Sydney library was offering a free session on tax preparation for self-employed professionals. The weather was good for March, she could pick up some supplies, and the cost of the trip would be tax-deductible. Reason enough for a weekend away. She could return that night, but it would be late, and there was snow in the forecast, so she'd booked a hotel in Sydney.

When she stopped at the Co-op to drop off Cerebus, Susan and Wendy had teased her about going to Sydney for a dirty weekend. Marianna had laughed at that, but somewhere around Cape Smokey she wondered if that might be a good idea. Replace the memory of Dylan in her bed with someone different. But not, she decided, during an overnight in Sydney. In the summer, perhaps, with someone visiting the campground.

She made good time, despite the extra driving since the St. Ann's ferry wasn't running. Driving through town, she considered the fast-food options, but realized she didn't crave that fare anymore. She drove to the hotel, checked in, then found a small new restaurant that had received great reviews online. If it deserved it, she'd add her own review, aware of how much attention tourists paid to these.

While she waited for her food, she recalled the review Dylan had left for her campground, last fall. He had not mentioned anything about the rain and washed-out road. He talked about the fabulous sunsets, the northern lights, the great beach, the fantastic hike, and the friendly proprietor. She had responded with a thank-you note on the site.

Her appetizer of steamed mussels in garlic sauce arrived, elegantly presented and deliciously fragrant. The homemade bun was a perfect accompaniment. Crusty on the outside, buttery soft on the inside. This place will do well, she thought, and she'd recommend it. She looked around to see if they displayed brochures of local attractions, hoping to do a brochure swap. The rest of the lunch was equally appealing, and after lunch she enjoyed a stroll along the harbour boardwalk. It was sunny, and warm out of the wind.

That afternoon she visited the local shopping centres, picking up some bulk food items and paint. She spotted a new lingerie store and found several appealing designs. The matronly clerk at the register praised her selection. "These will look lovely on you, dear." She glanced down at Marianna's left hand. "The men love these, you know."

"My last," she was not sure how to refer to him, "boyfriend said I'm not the lacy bra type."

"Well dear, his loss. I don't know any woman who doesn't like a lacy bra." Her voice dropped. "I found out that even lesbians like lacy bras. Well, not all of them, but some of them."

"Some of the bras, or some of the lesbians?" asked Marianna.

The sales lady looked confused to a moment, then laughed, understanding Marianna had made a joke, but not quite getting it. "Oh, yes, I see."

Walking back to the hotel, she noticed a new-and-used bookstore in a previously vacant storefront. She stepped in, greeted the large white cat that glanced at her from an upper shelf, was greeted by a young woman at the register, and looked over the large selection. She picked out a couple of thrillers from a bookcase labelled "Maritime Authors." She wasn't sure when she'd get to reading them but purchasing them would support local authors and the business.

"Congratulations on opening. You have a great selection. You should do well, especially when the tourists start arriving," said Marianna.

"Thanks. That's what they tell me."

"Marianna." She held out her hand. "I run a campground up past the Cabot Trail."

"Lizzy. Nice to meet you." She shook Marianna's hand. "I'd like to get up there sometime, when it's warmer, but before the busy season. Need a break, though. I've been in the store every day since I got here."

"Where are you from, then?"

"My store used to be in Hamilton. Near Toronto, Ontario."

"I know where that is. I lived in Toronto for a bit myself. What brought you out here?"

"Would you believe true love? Sounds silly, but about a year ago I sold a book online to a guy that lives here. We chatted, and one thing led to another." She blushed. "It was easier for me to move here than for him to move to Ontario. The rent's cheaper and most of my sales are online anyway."

* * *

Marianna was late to arrive at the evening library seminar, having lingered too long reading a new-to-her book in her hotel room. There were only empty chairs left in the front row, but a sympathetic library staff member pulled a chair from a stack at the back wall. The librarian was welcoming the attendees and reminding them of the many other services offered by the library. Then she introduced the presenter for the tax seminar.

"As you all know, Jack passed on last year, and we weren't sure who might do this session for us, but I'm delighted to announce we've found a new local tax professional who's willing to take a few hours at the busiest time of the year to help us out. Now this gentleman does sound like a come-from-away, thanks to too many years in Toronto—what a sin."

Marianna's heart pounded. It couldn't be. "But he's a good Nova Scotia lad, born down Yarmouth way and settled in Baddeck some months now." She looked around and saw Dylan seated at the end of the front row. She was sure it was him, though she could only see the back of his head. "Not exactly seeing Cape Breton at its best, moving here in the winter, but we're glad he's here to give this session, our annual Tax Preparation for Small Businesses. We need all the help we can get. Please welcome Dylan Felder."

Dylan stood up and walked to the podium. There was polite applause. The lady next to Marianna leaned over and whispered, "Quite a hunk, dear. Not what I expected when they said there was a new accountant presenting." Marianna nodded, unable to speak. Dylan looked over the crowd, thanked everyone, and smiled. Marianna noticed him scanning the crowd, as if he was looking for someone. He caught Marianna's eye, looked away, then glanced back. He registered the shock on her face, and his face became more serious. He turned to his notes and advanced to the next slide. "Thanks everyone. First, a little about my qualifications, just so you know what I can and cannot answer."

Marianna considered leaving but decided that would be rude. It had been five months since his visit to the campground. He'd ended any connection between them. And she could use the information. She would stay to the end, politely greet him, and leave. Did she even have to greet him then? She'd never expected to see him again. That would have been much easier. And now he lived nearby. She'd probably see him in town again. She could be civil. It was absurd that he still aroused such emotion after so many months, when it had been just a few days acquaintance, and he had behaved so badly. But the past was distorted. The time together seemed longer, the time apart shorter, and the betrayal fuzzy and distant.

She looked down at her notes, reminding herself of the tax questions she had, and focused on the content, not the speaker. He was polished, professional, and comfortable addressing the group, and it was clear he knew some of the audience. "No, Jerry, the new small business tax exemption would not be available for you, since you've been running the tour as a sole proprietorship for six years. But there are other advantages of incorporation. Probably still a good idea."

Ninety minutes later, the librarian thanked everyone for attending, and reminded the group that the building closed in half an hour. Marianna had covered three pages with notes, and while his presentation had answered all her questions, looking at her notes she realized she had a new one. She finished jotting down the question, then looked up. A line of people wanting to talk to Dylan had formed. Marianna looked back at her notes and reviewed them to make sure she could read her quick jottings. The section on allowable expenses was full of scribbles, and she tried to clarify the main points. A shadow moved across her notebook, and she looked up.

"Hello Marianna. It's nice to see you again."

"What are you doing here?" she blurted. "I mean, I'm surprised to see you. Why didn't you say you'd moved here?"

"I was going to tell you as soon as I figured out how."

He sat down beside her. "Do you have time for a drink? I'd like to toast my first customer and tell her how much I appreciate her, her business, even if it wasn't entirely her choice."

"I'm not your customer anymore."

"No. But you were my first customer, and the most important one. And if you are wondering why I sold your loan, I can explain that. But it's a long story, and the library closes soon. Do you have time for a drink?"

She wanted to say no. She should say no. That would be keeping things professional. But professionals can meet for a drink to review their business deals, she rationalized. Why had he moved here? "I have a little time. One drink."

"Thanks." He stood and offered his hand to help her up. She accepted it.

"Given the temperature, I think hot chocolate would be suitable."

"Benson's? Via the boardwalk?" She nodded, wondering how he knew about Benson's, and how often he'd been there—and with whom.

They walked in silence along the boardwalk to the giant fiddle at the empty cruise ship dock. A light snow fell, flakes drifting in gentle winds. The winds faded but the snow increased as they turned up to the street and entered Benson and Lucy's Beans and Leaves.

"This place should make you feel at home," she said, trying to lighten the mood.

"I've only been to Sydney a couple of times."

"No, I meant it's trendy and chic, like something you'd find on Queen Street in Toronto. In case you're missing that."

"Well, I have been missing something," he said, but did not smile. She was not sure how to respond. They placed their orders and waited, perched on stools at a high table in a quiet corner. The hot chocolate arrived, with whipped cream and chocolate sprinkles on top.

"So, you moved here." She wanted to know why, and what, if anything, he expected from her. His presence raised many possibilities, not all of them good.

* * *

She looked suspicious, and Dylan could not blame her. "I owe you countless apologies," he said. "I deceived and misled you about the purpose of my visit. But I never lied about my affection for you. And more than apologies, I owe you thanks. You showed me a way of life I'd forgotten, values I thought I didn't need, and possibilities I was too stupid to consider. Thanks to you, I visited my sister, and she helped me down the road you set me on." One of her hands was resting on the table. Dylan reached to cover it with his, but she pulled her hand back.

"What road is that?" Marianna asked.

"As I expected, I was fired even before I got back to Toronto. I had been wanting to set up my own company. I had a location in mind, appropriate for the type of business and clients I wanted to attract. With the collapse of the deal to buy your campground, I didn't have the money to do that, but I no longer had the desire to do that either. Instead, I sold my condo, as you know, sent a few emails, called in a few favours, and set up a company to restructure and refinance small businesses burdened with predatory loans, or wanting to grow but denied conventional financing. My sister-in-law was my second client. I helped her set up her own business, and now provide advice and tax help, in exchange for a share of the ownership and profits."

"What does she do?"

"She has a mobile forklift repair business. I visit once every month or two, and it's doing well. Since most of my work is online, I can work while visiting her, and live anywhere. I run a virtual office out of Toronto, since lots of people expect that, but I also hung out a shingle at my place in Baddeck."

"Why Baddeck?"

Dylan relaxed. At least her tone was neutral, not angry. "I looked around, on the way back from your place, and liked what I saw. I wasn't sure where I would settle, but I knew I wanted to come home to Nova Scotia. Then one of my early clients, after you and my sister, had a crushing mortgage on a small roadside motel there. I figured it was a sign. The deal we worked out has me as the owner, with the former owner and his family as most of the staff. They are much happier with the steady income and regular hours. I renovated a room to be a home for me, and I've been renovating the other rooms, one at a time, to get exercise and work with my hands."

"Sounds like this is a permanent move."

"Yes."

She looked displeased.

"It's nothing to do with us—you. This is where I belong." He wanted to reassure her that he had no expectations resuming their relationship, but that seemed presumptuous. But her puzzled expression turned out to be business related, not personal.

"We're going to be competitors in the hospitality business? That's why you sold my loan? Conflict of interest?"

"We won't be competitors. I'll be serving people who want to stay at motels, while you get campers. And we are several hours apart. At least a day, really, if you allow time to explore the trail. We might have some overlap in customers, especially if we recommend each other—carry each other's brochures." He searched her eyes for interest and saw a flicker of something he read as encouraging.

"The day I left the campground, I suggested we could continue things if I moved out here. That was presumptuous of me. Very rude. Like I said, I owe you countless apologies. It would be unfair of me to ask you out if you owed me money."

"You sold the loan so I wouldn't owe you money."

"Yes. I can't use our business relationship as an excuse to stay in touch, and you don't owe me any money. You don't owe me anything."

"How did you sell the loan without the terms getting changed? Are you guaranteeing it?"

"No. I took a loss selling it, but you don't owe me anything for that either. The loss is beneficial for my taxes, so I come out ahead. And, uh, if I ask you out, there's no pressure."

"Are you going to ask me out?"

Dylan tried to gauge whether her question was optimistic or wary. Her face gave nothing away.

"Since leaving my job and moving here, my life has been much better. The icing on the cake would be time with a smart, hardworking, independent, and beautiful woman—the one who inspired me to change. Yes, I'm going to ask you out. Right now. Would you like to go out for dinner? Tomorrow night, if you're staying in town. If not, any night that works for you."

Marianna took a sip of her hot chocolate, without answering him, then looked out the window. Had he misread her interest? To avoid saying something to make things worse, he sipped his hot chocolate, getting a whipped cream moustache.

Marianna turned back to him. "Cute moustache."

"You have one too." She was joking, not angry. That was good, wasn't it? Or was she not taking him seriously? He tried a neutral subject.

"How's Cerebus doing?"

"He's fine. Hasn't wandered off again. I bought a radio tracker collar in case he does."

"Good."

She looked out the window again, then turned back to him. "How have you found the winter?"

"You were right. It was brutal for a while. But I survived."

"This winter's been mild, so far. It's not over until the snow melts."

He tried to see if that flicker of interest was still in her eyes. He did not see it. It was time to say goodbye. He stood up.

"It was great to see you again. Good luck with the upcoming season."

* * *

"Wait," she called, as he walked away. He came back and sat down. "I need to say something." He was nervous, not smiling, but when he'd smiled this evening, during the workshop and their chat there, his smile was deeper than she'd seen before. His voice was more relaxed. The cockiness on display when he'd arrived at the campground, and which had still been present when he left, was gone, replaced by the quiet confidence of someone comfortable with themselves. Perhaps because he was being honest with her, in a way he'd never been at the campground. At least until the last morning, and she wasn't sure he was being honest then. Now she needed to be honest with him, and herself.

"The day you left, I said some things that were, that I'm not proud of. I was angry."

"It's okay." Dylan put his hand on hers. "All things I deserved."

"Maybe. But you were trying to do the right thing. It took me a few months to realize that. I am sorry for the way I reacted."

"Apology accepted. I'm sorry for what I was doing, and the crude offer I made."

"Apology accepted." They shared a smile.

"You said some things too," she said. "You said you'd like us to try to continue our .... I'm not sure what to call it."

"I don't care what you call it." He gripped her hand, and she squeezed back.

She took a sip of her drink, gathering courage for what she wanted to say. After he'd left, and her anger subsided, and she stopped telling herself how ridiculous it was, she had realized she'd fallen in love with him. She wouldn't have thought it possible, but it had happened to her mum. Seeing him again tonight, suddenly everything was possible. She opened her mouth, but he started talking.

"I need to say something too. Have to be totally honest. I don't know how it happened so fast, but maybe how fast it happened is why it took me a while to realize what had happened. I love you. If you don't want me to ever say that again, I won't. If you never want to speak to me again after tonight, I will respect that. If we meet again by chance, like tonight, I will be polite and civil, but otherwise leave you alone. I will never stop loving you, but if you do not want any relationship, I will respect that. If you think a relationship is possible but are not sure—and after just a few days, I can appreciate you being hesitant—then let's go slow. One date at a time."

He'd been looking at his hot chocolate while talking, but he looked up, hoping to see a positive response. She watched his expression turn to joy as he read her face.

"It's too soon to be making declarations of love," said Marianna. "I need some time to process my feelings about you, about us. But I do know I've missed you. A lot. *Did I actually say process my feelings?* "I like the idea of going slow."

She leaned towards him and tilted her face up as his came down to hers. The kiss was hesitant, then passionate. They stopped when the baristas clapped.

"So, is that a yes to the dinner date tomorrow?"

A regular date could be fun, Marianna thought, though weren't they beyond that? Cerebus was staying with Susan and Wendy, so she could drive back later, or even stay another day in Sydney, but she wanted to get home, and preferred driving the country roads in daylight. "I'm heading back tomorrow afternoon, so dinner's out. Perhaps lunch?"

He grinned. "Thank you. I can meet you somewhere or pick you up."

"Can you be back in town by noon?"

"I'm staying at the Delta here tonight. With the snow, I didn't want to risk Kellys Mountain. Not sure if that makes me a nervous come-from-away or a wise local."

"I'd say a wise local, but then I'm almost a come-from-away myself."

They each drained their drinks.

"So, until tomorrow then?" she asked. He was in town, and she was in town. She was having second thoughts about going slow. That's the sensible thing to do, she told herself.

"May I walk you back to your hotel? But I should warn you, I might ask for a goodnight kiss."

"I might grant that," she teased. "I might even invite you up to my room. But I'm at the Days Inn. The Delta's nicer and has a pool. Can I still claim my room as a business expense if I don't sleep in it tonight?" *Forget going slow.*

"Yes. Absolutely. I'd be entirely comfortable putting that in your tax return, if you hire me to do your taxes." He finished his hot chocolate, restoring his moustache.

"I guess I can't ask for the taxes for free since you don't hold the loan anymore." She wiped the whipped cream and chocolate off his face.

"Marianna, I'm happy to be your accountant, handyman, dog walker, and campground washroom-cleaner, but there's something else I'd like to be tonight." He leaned forward and whispered in her ear. "Your lover."

She whispered back, "I'd like that."

23

∿

Chapter 23

A year later

Marianna walked along the beach, enjoying the warmth and solitude, and looking forward to the stars promised by the clear sky. Even when the campground was close to capacity, as it had been several times over the summer, the beach was never crowded, and this afternoon the only activity was at the bottom of the stairs, behind her. She reached the eastern edge of her property, where a shale cliff met the sand, and turned back. A quiet walk along the beach, enjoying the surf and salt air, was just what she needed now. Not that she had any regrets. Dylan's acceptance of her solitary walks was further proof she'd made the right decision.

The wedding ceremony, this morning in the picnic shelter, had been more crowded than she expected. Everyone in the village had wanted to come, and Sheila reported hundreds of people watched the livestream. As uncomfortable as that was, it was great publicity, and three people had already emailed asking about holding their weddings at the campground. The casual lunch reception afterwards had meant endless handshakes and hugs from well-wishers. She'd been gracious, but grateful when people started to drift away.

Dinner was a lobster bake on the beach, for family and close friends. As quiet as it could be, with two children chasing and being chased by a dog. As Marianna grew closer, she could hear Susan's daughter, Wendy, warning Alison and Cole when they came too close to the water.

Cole complained. "We can swim. We wade in the water all the time."

"I'm glad you can swim, but your moms said you had to stay out of the water tonight."

Cole saw Marianna approaching. "Aunt Marianna, can we go in? Just our feet?"

"If your moms said no, then the answer's no."

"We should ask Uncle Dylan," said Cole. "He's mom Jennifer's big brother, so he can tell her what to do."

"No, he isn't," said Alison. "He's mom Jennifer's little brother, so she tells him what to do."

Marianna intervened. "Dylan and Jennifer are all grown up, and when brothers and sisters are all grown up, they are equal and never fight about anything."

"Do you have a brother?" asked Alison.

"No," she said, "but I have a great niece and nephew, and your mums are like my sisters now." Marianna saw Dylan beckoning them. "We should go to the table. Uncle Dylan says it's ready."

Last year there had been four of them at one table: Marianna and Dylan, celebrating the marriage of Barry and Sheila.

This year there were three tables of diners. Barry stood to make a toast.

"Sheila and I celebrated our honeymoon here, a year ago. Sure, it was a little rough at times, but marriage is like that. There might be days with no water," he winked at Marianna, "or your car gets washed away," he nodded at Dylan, "or the grocery store declines your credit card." Marianna saw Sheila blush. "Or, not to leave me out of it, you break your leg slipping on ice the day before you are leaving on a cruise. A free cruise! But so long as you have each other, and remember that, you'll get through it. And look at us now! The campground is in great shape, and my leg's completely healed." He danced a few steps of a jig, then raised his glass. "To the blessed couple." Everyone stood and clinked glasses.

Marianna's mother spoke up. "I can't be as eloquent as Barry, and I don't want to keep us from the delicious dinner, so I'll keep it short. Thank you, Dylan and Marianna, and good luck to you."

"My turn," said Jennifer. "Thank you, Marianna, for helping Dylan come home."

"Congratulations to both of you," said Susan. "We love what you are both doing to keep the tourists coming up here."

Lizzy, Marianna's new friend from the bookstore in Sydney, stood up. "Dylan, you did the right thing, leaving Ontario and moving for love. Congratulations to both of you." She sat down, and exchange a kiss with her partner, Jose.

Marianna stood. "Thanks everyone. We are thrilled that you came to share this day with us, especially Mum for making the trip here. A year ago, I never dreamed I'd be married now. Thank you, everyone, for all you did to bring us together and help us along. Jennifer, Dylan told me you helped him figure things out. And thank you Susan and Wendy for not only taking care of the lobster bake but building me a fire pit. A fabulous wedding gift. And I know you offered to do the dishes but let me repeat that Dylan and I want to do them."

Dylan stood. "It's a funny story—."

"Enough talking," yelled Sheila, aiming her phone. "Let's see a kiss."

Marianna leaned over to Dylan for a light peck and whispered, "We're hungry."

"I'll keep this short, but I have to say something. I have learned a lot about friends and family in the past year, thanks to this wonderful woman." Marianna smiled and looked down as the others applauded her. Dylan took her hand, and spoke again, slower and deeper. "Thank you, Marianna, for showing me the stars," he waved at the darkening sky, "and for being the brightest star in my universe." Everyone touched glasses, and the couple kissed, more passionately this time. So much public kissing today, thought Marianna, eager to settle in for the night.

Everyone sat down except Susan and her daughter, who brought the steaming foil packages to each plate. Sorry you're missing this, Grandma, Marianna thought, but we're using your dishes and silver, so it's like you are here in spirit. Dylan told her mother how impressed he'd been with this meal last year. So much had happened since then.

* * *

Dylan had moved into her house at the beginning of July, after commuting for visits most weekends during the spring. The campground was busy, more than half full for the holiday weekend, but Dylan had convinced her to go for a hike and leave the campground in the care of her summer employees.

"No one's checking in or out today, I helped Riley finish cleaning early, and she and her brother have everything under control. We'll be back by dinner. You deserve a break, and some quiet time on this gorgeous day."

She didn't argue with that. They hiked up the mountain, enjoyed lunch in the clearing on the ridge, and lay on the grass in the shade, listening to the creaks and murmurs of the trees in the cooling breeze.

Dylan spoke. "Would you be interested in a proposal?"

She sat up. "I beg your pardon?"

"I've finished renovating the motel rooms, so I don't need to be there anymore. I'm here at least every weekend. Suppose I stayed here? I'd pay room and board, of course. I work in the second bedroom when I'm here, and I could set that up to be my office and hang out space, out of your way."

He sounded like he was joking, but she was not sure. "And you'd make money renting out your room at the motel." She pulled a dandelion and threw it at his chest. "Always about making money."

Dylan sat up, picked up the dandelion, and placed it in her hand. "True. It would be good for me financially, but also good for you. How about I sweeten the deal? I'll use some of the extra money to bring high-speed internet to the campground. I'll used the saved commuting time to build those cabins. And I'll offer to marry you, because being with you is more important to me than anything else." He reached into his jeans pocket and pulled out a blue velvet pouch. From it, he extracted a ring and offered it to her.

She looked the diamond solitaire ring. It gleamed in the sun. It was an old design, featuring art deco styling with a bezel cut.

"It was my grandmother's," he said. "Jennifer gave Mum's to Tina and was keeping this one for me. I didn't even know."

"It's beautiful," she said.

"Is that a yes?"

"You haven't actually asked. Let's hear it. And it better include that room and board payment you mentioned."

He laughed and made some flowery speech she could not remember. That led to giggles, and tickles, and they'd ended up making love on a blanket, her wearing nothing but the ring, and "in full view of anyone in a boat down there," as Dylan said.

* * *

Marianna and Dylan stood at the sink. The remnants of the wedding dinner were stacked on the counter and in bins, all carried up in one trip, thanks to their guests, who had hastened off to their cabins or home. Cole and Alison had insisted on taking Cerebus to their cabin for the night, and he was happy to go with them.

"Just like a year ago," Dylan said. "The first time we kissed."

"Except for this." Marianna raised her hand. The ring blazed as it caught the setting sun.

"Same colour as your hair," said Dylan, running his hand through her hair.

"Some day you'll have to tell me about this," said Marianna, tracing his scar, and running her fingers across his lips.

"It can wait."

"So can the dishes."

About the Author

Tim Covell
Photo by Nicola Davison

Tim Covell was born on Canada's west coast, lived in central Canada, and now lives on the east coast. He writes fiction and non-fiction, including romance, short humour, poetry, biography, software instructions, and journal articles. He holds degrees in English Literature, Film Studies, and Canadian Studies, and researches film classification and censorship. http://www.covell.ca